"What are you doing here?"

David said the words more harshly than he should have, but he didn't want to have her here in this place that was his sanctuary.

"I'm sorry. I'll leave." Callie turned, then stumbled on the uneven ground.

He grabbed her to steady her. The warmth of her skin was like a door opening to a room with a crackling fireplace and the heady scent of welcome.

David had been cold for a long, long time. He felt the stir of a sense of possibility, the slightest tendril of hope. "Callie..."

Her lips parted, and he leaned toward her. It would be so easy to forget, to cast out doubts, to lose himself....

David backed away. He could not afford to trust her. Feeling Callie's eyes on him every step down the road, he cursed himself. And fate.

Dear Reader,

I believe to the depths of my soul that love is the most powerful force on the planet. I didn't discover romance novels until I was grown and raising my family, but though I came late to the party, I have the utmost admiration for what Harlequin celebrates—not simply love, but honor, loyalty, courage and compassion, a core faith in the goodness of human nature, all values that strengthen us in our daily lives and help us endure the rough patches.

I feel very fortunate to be one of those granted the privilege of sharing my stories with you. To be a part of the compelling and noteworthy legacy of Harlequin Superromance, to join a tradition formed by stellar authors such as Judith Arnold, Marisa Carroll, Margot Early and others is a true honor. I first came to Harlequin Superromance during the time of the remarkable and innovative Paula Eykelhof and am fortunate today to have the pleasure of working with Wanda Ottewell, who's not only a lovely and fun person but whose keen editorial insights sincerely impress me.

It was a lucky day in my life when I became a part of Harlequin's grand adventure. Please join me in saluting a remarkable achievement while looking forward to many more years of wonderful stories— happy 60th Anniversary, Harlequin!

All my best,

Jean Brashear

The Man She Once Knew
Jean Brashear

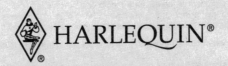

HARLEQUIN®

TORONTO • NEW YORK • LONDON
AMSTERDAM • PARIS • SYDNEY • HAMBURG
STOCKHOLM • ATHENS • TOKYO • MILAN • MADRID
PRAGUE • WARSAW • BUDAPEST • AUCKLAND

Recycling programs
for this product may
not exist in your area.

ISBN-13: 978-0-373-71595-4

THE MAN SHE ONCE KNEW

www.eHarlequin.com

Printed in U.S.A.

ABOUT THE AUTHOR

Three RITA® Award nominations, a *Romantic Times BOOKreviews* Series Storyteller of the Year and numerous other awards have all been huge thrills for Jean, but hearing from readers is a special joy. She would not lay claim to being a true gardener like Bella, but her houseplants are thriving. She does play guitar, though, knows exactly how it feels to have the man you love craft a beautiful piece of furniture with his own hands…and has a special fondness for the scent of wood shavings.

Jean loves to hear from readers, either via e-mail at her Web site www.jeanbrashear.com, or Harlequin's Web site, www.eHarlequin.com, or by postal mail at P.O. Box 3000 #79, Georgetown, TX 78627-3000.

Books by Jean Brashear

To Ercel, whose strong shoulders have always
been there for me to lean on.
Your love is my life's greatest blessing.

Acknowledgments

Kelly Brashear Kitchens, lawyer extraordinaire, has
been a godsend during the writing of this book, not
only for her knowledge of Georgia criminal law but for
her willingness to let me spin out tales while yanking
me back to reality in the kindest of manners...all with
response times that were a lifesaver!
Any errors made or liberties taken are
most assuredly my own.

My thanks to Wanda Ottewell for bringing me back
home to Harlequin Superromance and being a delightful
presence at the doorway when I arrived!

CHAPTER ONE

Blue Ridge Mountains
Georgia

THE CHAPEL WAS wall-to-wall strangers. All the better.

Callie Hunter had no desire to be connected to the hell-raising fourteen-year-old she'd been, bottle-black, scarlet-tipped hair, piercings and all. That summer she'd been banished to Oak Hollow by her mother was one she'd shoved to the back of the closet.

One stiletto-clad foot swung impatiently from her crossed knees. As soon as the service was over, she was out of here. Only her feelings for Miss Margaret, as her great-aunt Margaret Jennings was known, could have dragged Callie back to the mountain of Georgia. Not one time in the sixteen years since she'd left had she returned. Memories of shame and sorrow clogged the valleys and hollows of this Smoky Mountain landscape. Agonizing reminders lurked on each rounded peak, waiting to pounce on her with the stealth of a wildcat.

Faint murmuring began to creep through the congregation like fog stealing over a riverbank, spilling up the nearest rise of land, and Callie could only assume someone had, after all, recognized her. She steeled herself. The funeral would be over soon. She'd deposit a generous donation with the minister and jump into her car. Be back in Philadelphia before morning, burrowed safely in her real life where she balanced the scales of justice, put the bad guys away. Where Callie Hunter was a rising star in the District Attorney's office, with plans to one day run for election and replace her boss.

Assuming, that is, that she could reverse the damage she'd done to herself in the high-profile case she'd recently lost, a severe blow to the reputation of the wunderkind known in the tough Philly press as Lady Justice for her ardent prosecution of crime and her record conviction rate. She itched to get home and prove herself. Her job was her life; every second she had to be away during this critical period was torture.

The murmuring grew loud enough to drown out the organ music that she found creepy. When mutters rose to a crescendo behind her, Callie gave up and turned, only to discover that no one was paying her an iota of attention.

Instead, every eye appeared to be focused on a man just entering at the back. Callie shifted to see who he was.

When she did, her heart stuttered.

No. It could not be. She examined the tall, powerful frame for signs of the boy she hadn't let herself think of in years.

The man's gaze flickered over her and onward. His stony expression never wavered.

She was seized by an impulse to get closer, to see if she was mistaken. Should she talk to him? But what on earth would she say?

He disappeared into a back pew before she could decide, and Callie turned to face the front again.

Just as well. There was nothing for her here. She couldn't wait to be gone.

WHY WAS HE HERE? Hadn't fifteen years in prison taught him hard lessons about caution?

Regardless of how intense those months together had been, he and Callie had parted ways as though strangers. There had been nothing to hold them together, it turned out, after the roller coaster of emotion, the drama and heartache. A boy's damn-fool notion of honor had exploded in his face, had blasted his future to bits.

What had he expected to feel? He had no idea who she was anymore, except that she was beautiful—man, was she ever. The badly dyed black hair had given way to the natural blond he'd seen only at her roots, the profusion of curls she'd so often derided were now a shiny, straight cap. She'd grown a good three inches, he guessed, no longer that tiny rebel.

No rebel at all, from what he'd heard. A prosecutor—fate sure had a nasty sense of humor. Their role reversals appeared to be complete.

Didn't matter. Nothing mattered really, only biding his time, doing what he could for the one person who still held a claim on his shriveled heart. If not for his mother's need of him, he'd never have set foot in Oak Hollow again. The road pulled at him, the longing to disappear, to start over somewhere, anywhere that no one knew him.

He'd come from good stock; his father had died rescuing two hikers from a fall. However desperate and defeated his mother was now, she once had raised a boy single-handed, struggled to keep body and soul together for both of them. An excellent student—particularly at math and science—with ambitions of being a pilot and astronaut, David had grown up under the caring eyes of an impoverished town where hardly anyone made it to college.

She'd taken in sewing at night after long days of waiting tables to be sure he had basketball shoes and football uniforms. She'd grown vegetables and raised chickens to keep food on the table.

He wondered if she thought any of the struggle had been worth it when she'd been writing letters to a prison instead of the university where he was to have received a football scholarship.

He'd served his time, and he was supposed to be free now. Instead he was back in Oak Hollow, despised by everyone but his mother for dealing a mortal blow to the dreams of a town that had expected him to succeed for all of them.

Tough. The townspeople needed to get their own dreams.

The organ music swelled, yanking David from his musings. Just as well—the past was a hostile country to visit. He glanced toward the front and realized that there was nothing to say to the woman Callie had grown into. He should never have come.

Before the ushers began leading the mourners out, David Langley slipped into the shadows and through the side door.

With long strides, he left the past where it belonged.

CHAPTER TWO

"MS. HUNTER?" Outside the chapel, a stooped man with a weathered face paused before her. "I'm sorry for your loss."

She accepted his handshake. "Thank you." She let go, eager to leave.

But he lingered. "I'm Albert Manning. I need to see you at my office as soon as you're ready."

"Excuse me?"

"I'm sorry. Miss Margaret's death has addled me. I'm her attorney." His forlorn expression spoke of a deeper sense of loss than for a mere client, however. "There are issues we must address as soon as possible."

"What?" Callie frowned. "But I'm leaving. Right now," she added.

"It would be a kindness if you could stay one night, at least. Miss Margaret's house is ready for you. As you know, there are no hotels or motels in Oak Hollow."

It would be a kindness. How had she forgotten Southern pleasantries so quickly? There was not a man she'd ever met in Philly who would talk like that.

"But I—" *Have to get back immediately. I have a reputation to save. A future to secure.*

"Please, Ms. Hunter—Callie, if I may. Miss Margaret was very proud of you and spoke of you so often that I feel I know you."

Shame left a bitter taste in Callie's mouth. She had abandoned her great-aunt years ago as she fled the painful memories of her time here. "Mr. Manning, I really must return to Philadelphia and my work. Can't we handle this on the phone?" Even if her great-aunt had made some sort of bequest, what could there be to deal with, really? Miss Margaret had lived hand-to-mouth in her small frame house.

"I'm afraid I must insist that you stay, at least until tomorrow." His tone was gentle but adamant. "There are issues that are inappropriate for me to bring up here."

There was actually no reason she had to leave today except her own need to save her reputation. Her boss, Gerald Parks, had ordered her to take an extended leave, utilizing some of her unused vacation time in lieu of a suspension after she'd skirted the line trying to win her last case. What he omitted—but she knew all too well— was that his concern was not for her but for his own reelection campaign.

Even if she agreed to remain here tonight, she didn't want to be at Miss Margaret's, not when memories lurked in every corner. "I'll drive over to the county seat and spend the night, then come back tomorrow to meet with you."

"There's no reason to make that hour drive. Miss Margaret was set on you staying in the house. She asked specifically."

Callie did not appreciate feeling cornered. *I don't want to* was her only defense, however, and she would not admit to a soul why that was. "Mr. Manning—"

"Please," he said, eyes soft with compassion. "She knew staying there would be difficult, but it was important to her. She loved you, Ms. Hunter. She blamed herself for what happened."

How much did he know? Callie was desperate to turn and run.

If you've become that easy to rattle, how do you expect to beat what's facing you back in Philly?

"All right." She squared her shoulders. It was just a house, a collection of boards and nails. And only one night. "Where do I find the key? What time shall we meet? I'd like to make it early so I can get on the road. I have a thirteen-hour drive ahead of me."

He smiled. "This is Oak Hollow, Ms. Hunter. We don't lock our houses. The electricity and water are on, and I took the liberty of having my wife stock the refrigerator for you." He took her hand in his. "Thank you. It would have meant a lot to Miss Margaret to have you there. Shall we meet at nine, then? I'm up earlier, of course, but I like to take my time these days. No reason to get in a rush."

Time waits for no one, she wanted to retort. *And Miss Margaret is dead. She won't care.* But she bit her tongue and simply nodded. "Nine it is. How do I find you?"

"It's the yellow frame house catty-corner from town hall," he explained. "You know where that is, right?"

She nodded. "I'll find it." She turned to go.

"Oh, and Ms. Hunter, I am sorry you had to be subjected to that display earlier. He had no business being there when decent people were burying their dead. He shouldn't be in Oak Hollow at all, folks think."

She revolved slowly. "Are you speaking of David Langley? Was that him in the chapel?"

"He was." His face was tight with disapproval. "We don't hold with criminals in our midst. If he bothers you at all, just speak up. The sheriff is keeping an eye on him."

Callie's eyes popped. "Criminal? *David?*"

"Miss Margaret never told you? I would have thought, given your—" His face was reddening. "I mean, since he and you—" He worried at the brim of his straw hat.

She rushed past his fumbling. "Told me what?"

He looked away, then back. "I suppose you'll find out anyhow," he said almost to himself. "David Langley just got out of prison three months ago after serving fifteen years."

"*Prison?* For what?" Callie couldn't wrap her mind around the idea of David being a criminal, but the buzzing at the chapel and his unyielding expression were making more sense now.

"Why, for murder, of course—only he got off easy and was convicted of manslaughter instead."

She couldn't help her gasp. "That's impossible. David would never—"

"Oh, yes, ma'am, he surely did, but I'm sorry—I should not have brought up such an unpleasant topic, especially when you're in mourning." His jaw clenched.

"I will make certain that he doesn't come near you again, rest assured. Now let me escort you to the car."

He made as if to grasp her elbow, but Callie strode ahead briskly toward the sedan where the funeral director waited patiently. Mr. Manning followed, tipped his hat and said goodbye.

Once in the car on the way to the cemetery, Callie let herself feel the impact of what she'd heard. She'd dreaded returning to Oak Hollow, dreaded brushing up against her past. She'd intended to cruise as lightly as possible into and out of the site of the most painful period of her life.

But if she'd known what she would encounter and the havoc it would create inside her—

Nothing on this earth could have forced her back.

DAVID STRAIGHTENED with a groan. Rolled his shoulders and stretched his back, then lifted the hoe and headed for the toolshed at the back of his mother's garden. When he was growing up, the garden had been lush and green, its bounty plenty to keep them over the winter while providing extra that David sold at a makeshift stand on the highway.

The plot his mother had patiently cultivated for years had lain fallow for a long time, perhaps ever since he'd been gone. He wasn't sure why he was bothering with it now, except that he'd seen her wistful gaze land on it often as she stared out her kitchen window.

The smell of the dirt had drawn him in first, one restless night soon after his arrival. He'd craved to lose himself in the oblivion of slumber, but he couldn't get used to the quiet. Prison was never silent, and the sound of the frogs outside had been as startling as gunshots. He'd learned to slide beneath the layers of guards talking, inmates snoring or groaning, new prisoners crying…and more furtive, desperate sounds he never wanted to hear again in his life. Then there was the darkness. Even with a full moon, as had been the case when he'd first returned, his room was dark as pitch compared to the harsh glare of the prison fluorescents that never fully dimmed.

He'd encountered the garden on one of those uneasy nights, leaping from the bed that had been his as a teen—the same bed where he'd once conjured up dreams of the life he'd live, the places he'd see, the difference he'd make.

The bed was too soft for him now. Too much a torture, stinking as it did of his failures. He'd taken up sleeping on the floor instead, often outside on the screened-in porch at the back of the small house. He couldn't get enough of fresh air, of room to move. Some nights he took off down the country road in front of his mother's house, running five, six, ten miles at a time, trying to sweat out fifteen years of misery.

And the present, as devoid of hope, in some ways, as each day behind bars.

He stifled the urge to throw the hoe like a javelin, to damage something, hurt something, to shatter the paper-thin wall with the rage that he pushed down and down and down—

He stopped in his tracks, dust motes drifting in the air, sweating and shaking with the effort of keeping it all inside. Why did Callie have to show up now and make him face exactly how far he'd fallen?

Lock it down. Kill the fury with your bare hands. If you don't get a grip, son, you'll be in here forever. The advice of fellow prisoner Sam Eakins, eighty years old if he was a day, had saved him in those early weeks when David's gut-churning fear had become a smoldering rage.

He had to stop thinking about what might have been. It couldn't matter that he had a crap job, cleaning up after drunks in a bar where patrons like Mickey Patton seldom missed an opportunity to jab at him, to spill a beer purposely on a freshly cleaned floor. To relish that David was cleaning toilets when he should have been flying a jet and wearing medals.

He had a job he badly needed, the only work anyone would give him. There was so much to be done around his mother's place, chores that she'd left neglected as her health declined. Until David had returned, he'd had no idea how impoverished her circumstances were, worse even than when she'd been newly widowed and responsible for a child.

If the roof over her head wasn't to fall down, the repair was up to him, and materials cost money. He'd sent most of his pitiful prison pay to her, but obviously it hadn't gone nearly far enough.

He stepped outside, washed off at the faucet and spotted his mother moving about in the kitchen, preparing his supper. He stared down at the hands that resembled his father's, then reached into his pocket and fingered the knife he had reclaimed from the small desk in his bedroom. His hands were rusty from years of disuse, but each day they itched a little more to resume the carving his father had taught him.

When the police had come to arrest him, he'd left the knife behind so it wouldn't be confiscated in jail. His fingers had gone blind after that, no longer able to create beauty or humor from only a stick, a block of wood. The last carving he'd completed before prison was one he wasn't ready to see yet.

He flexed his hands, his father's hands, then closed his fingers one by one into a fist.

No. Not yet. Until he could carve with the rage purged from his heart, he would leave the knife unopened.

David shook himself like a dog shedding rain.

Lock it down. Get a grip.

CALLIE HALTED two steps into the kitchen. Unbelievably, the small, scrubbed-to-an-inch-of-its-life house still smelled of the lavender water Miss Margaret used to iron her sheets, underlaid by frying bacon, homemade bread and a million or so cups of mint tea. She expected the older woman to pop around the corner any second.

By rote, Callie had entered the back door from the driveway. The front door was only for company, Miss Margaret had told her that first day. Callie was family, she'd insisted, however little Callie could believe back then that she belonged anywhere, especially in this warm refuge.

Callie glanced out the picture window that had been Miss Margaret's pride and joy, the one that gave her great-aunt a good view of the backyard she'd labored so many hours to create. Oh, she'd tended the front and sides, as well—weeds were not tolerated, and she'd had an eagle's eye for the slightest up-cropping—but the back was where her heart was planted. Vegetable garden off in the right-hand corner, roses lining the left. In between lay her rock garden, an exotic Southwestern creation as out of place in these ancient, rounded green mountains as Miss Margaret would have been in the desert.

I do believe I was a cowgirl in another life, she would say. *On my one trip to Los Angeles by train, I saw the desert for the first time and something in my soul expanded.* A look of intense regret would furrow her brow at the mention, but she never explained beyond one admonition. *Do not let your dreams pass you by, Callie Anne. When your heart tells you you're home, you listen, you hear me?*

Miss Margaret had been as foreign to a fourteen-year-old in full rebellion as a rose was to a coyote. Callie had rolled her eyes that first time, but after seeing the hurt she'd dealt to someone more harmless and innocent than Callie had ever been, she'd kept her cynicism to herself. Miss Margaret had been out of another century and older than dirt to boot in Callie's view, but a kindness in her smoothed off some of the edges of Callie's wild misery.

Miss Margaret had taken one look at her full-on Goth attire and pressed her lips together so hard they'd nearly disappeared. Just when Callie was ready to bolt, Miss Margaret had confided that two of her little earrings resembled a pair she'd wanted when she was young, except that her father would have sent her to the woodshed for piercing her ears. Ladies didn't do that, she'd said, then, with a puckish grin, she'd asked if Callie thought she was too old to try it now.

An astonished Callie had found herself offering to do the deed.

The Callie who stood in nearly the same spot now was surprised to find herself smiling.

Okay. She exhaled slowly. *It's only one night.*

She walked through the space, trailing her fingers over the old Tell City maple table and chairs in front of the picture window, the rocking recliner where Miss Margaret had sat to watch her television at night. Beside it stood a table groaning under the weight of not only a lamp but a good six months' worth of catalogs and magazines and, of course, Miss Margaret's ever-present King James Bible.

Callie stooped and started to pick up the Bible but faltered, her fingers instead drifting over the cracked leather binding, the gold cross worn nearly transparent.

Then she spotted the grocery list begun but not finished in that familiar spidery handwriting. She felt an urge to give way to grief she hadn't expected to feel for an old lady she hadn't seen since she left Oak Hollow.

Darkness encroached in this place of haunted memories, chipping away at Callie's carefully built defenses.

She leaped up so suddenly she stumbled. Quickly she

righted herself and charged through the house, flipping on the lights in every room.

Hoping to chase away the ghosts that still lurked.

ON HIS WAY TO WORK in his mother's ancient sedan, David took a detour. How many nights had he driven past the little house after Callie had left.

He turned the corner and saw light blazing from all the windows in a profligate display Miss Margaret would never have indulged—

No. She could not be staying.

Go away, Callie. He'd seen at the chapel that she hadn't known about him, but she would by now. Someone, probably lots of someones, would eagerly spill all the gruesome details to her.

He'd borne a lot, would have to bear more until his mother was gone and he was free at last. But seeing Callie, having her look at him the way everyone else did—

That, after all he'd survived, might finally break him.

Please, Callie. Go away and let me be.

CHAPTER THREE

MORNING'S LIGHT BANISHED the night's foolishness. Callie went about her preparations to leave, careful not to focus on any more details of this place in which she'd spent seven life-altering months. Other than the severely cut black suit she'd worn to the funeral, she had only the slacks and blouse she'd traveled in. Last night she'd washed out her lingerie and spread it out to dry on a towel bar while hanging up her suit in the closet of the room that was once hers.

She'd had no sleepwear either, and bare skin in Miss Margaret's house felt like a serious breach of manners. She couldn't bring herself to don anything as personal as one of the worn, soft nightgowns bearing the scent that was uniquely Miss Margaret's, however. Callie had compromised on a light robe and had dropped off to sleep early, surprising herself.

Now she combed through the cabinets looking for coffee she knew she wouldn't find. With a pang for the giant red-eye coffee—strong regular coffee spiked with espresso—she normally grabbed on her way to work in Philly, Callie had to settle for Miss Margaret's beloved

Earl Grey. No tea bags were tolerated in this house, so Callie found herself preparing tea Miss Margaret's way. There was something surprisingly soothing about engaging in the ritual she'd seen performed so often.

Miss Margaret didn't hold with mugs; a proper china cup was a must. When Callie opened the cabinet door, still painted cream and hinged with the hammered copper dating from the fifties, she spied the familiar china with its moss rose pattern, and for a second, Miss Margaret was all too real again. Callie ignored the tug, poured herself a cup, then carried it outside.

How many mornings had she awakened to find Miss Margaret in her garden wearing the old-fashioned sun-bonnet made by Miss Margaret's mother from flour sacks? How many conversations had they conducted there, the older woman's hands never idle while Callie fumbled to identify vegetable from weed?

She shook her head in amazement that at her age, her great-aunt had still planted, still managed to weed and water. *Gardening is life,* she'd say to Callie. *You learn everything you really need to know about the world right here.*

Who would wind up with this place? Who would care for it, love it and baby it as Miss Margaret had?

Callie bent to pluck one weed from the row of— Her brow furrowed. What were these plants? She rose abruptly. What did any of it matter? She would be gone this afternoon at the latest.

Oh, crap. Her stilettos were getting wet in the dew. Wouldn't her coworkers howl if they could see her beloved Manolos damp—wait. Was that dirt on the toes? She quickened her stride, lifting her foot high as she sought to spare the one indulgence in a sober wardrobe bought to ensure that, at only thirty, she was taken seriously in her position.

The reminder was a good one. She did not belong here, and it was no business of hers what happened with anyone or anything in Oak Hollow. Her life was elsewhere. She'd fought to make it so.

Thus resolved, she went inside, washed her cup and did a quick, impersonal check of the premises to be sure everything was squared away. Then, with a moment's hesitation over leaving the door unlocked, she got into her car and started it. In less than five minutes, she was parking across the street and down a bit from Albert Manning's law office. She walked swiftly, preoccupied with thoughts of what she would do first when she got back to Philly.

As she passed the post office, the door swung wide, and she nearly smacked right into it. A quick dodge to the side, and she tripped over a crack in the sidewalk.

A hand grabbed her arm and steadied her.

She lifted her head. "Excuse—" Every last thought vanished as she stared into a face she had once known intimately.

"David," she finally managed, her arm still tingling where he'd touched her, even through the fabric of her jacket. Whatever she might have meant to say dried up at the sight of him.

He only stared down at her, his face a mask.

He was big, so tall. She wasn't the tiny girl he'd known—she'd grown three and a half inches after she'd left here, five seven now. With her stilettos, she was an inch or so shy of six feet.

But he'd grown, too—six four, six five now at a guess—but it wasn't his height or even the layers of muscle that made the biggest impression on her.

It was his eyes. Once they had been mossy-green and soft, had spoken volumes to her, whether of love or heat or amusement. Patience had often lingered there, as well, far beyond what anyone would expect from someone so young.

When Callie had been exiled to Oak Hollow by a mother who wanted freedom to play with her latest sleazy boyfriend, she hadn't tried to hide her contempt for the hick ways of the locals. In return, she'd been ridiculed by the kids for her Goth attire and disliked by adults for her bad attitude. She'd pretended she didn't care, but David had found her in the woods one day, crying her eyes out. A compassionate soul, he'd talked to her and begun coming around, even though the other kids gave him a hard time.

She could accept all the changes she now saw in his frame, the new angles to his face, even the lines time and misery had carved into it.

But his eyes were a stranger's, hard and blank. Flat as though he and she had never met. As if they were nothing to each other.

Then astonishingly, he stepped around her without a word.

"David—" She reached out to stop him.

He shrugged her off and kept moving.

Callie turned and stared at his back. He'd once been so kind to her, so gentle. They'd shared something profound, yet he was pretending not to know her? Fury rode to the rescue. How dare he? She hadn't asked him to show up yesterday and set tongues wagging. She'd tried not to think of him last night, but he'd been one of the specters haunting her dreams. Now he disappeared from sight without a single glance back, as though she had no meaning to him.

Nothing could have put her back up quicker. She'd been judged wanting for too much of her life, and she had spent years of painstaking effort making sure she excelled, that no one could ever find her lacking again.

She stared in the direction he'd gone. *Fine. We're done. Good riddance.*

One hour. She would give the attorney one hour for whatever he needed to say.

Then Oak Hollow and all it had meant to her was over and done with.

KEEP WALKING. Get the hell out, get away from her before it's too late. David's long strides ate up the ground, the day's promising beauty lost on him as he barely kept himself from breaking into a run.

While her touch, that too-brief clasp, burned his skin like a brand.

When he was completely out of sight, he looked around to note that he'd wound up outside the fence of

Mickey Patton's welding shop, a junkyard of discarded pieces of farm equipment and rusted cars and trucks. Frantic barks pierced the air as the pit bulls Mickey kept for security lunged at the fence as though David were meat and they hadn't eaten in weeks. The pipe fence posts sang as they slammed into them, teeth bared, mouths foaming.

"Killer, Cutter—shut the hell up!" Patton emerged, face screwed up in displeasure.

Then he caught sight of David. "What are you doing here? Get your ass gone before I call Sheriff Carver on you and have you locked up again. You should be in there for life, you worthless son of a bitch."

David was no scared boy now, and though Patton was pure mean, David had faced down men in prison who made Patton look like a first-grader. He knew he could take the man in a fair fight, but Patton would never put himself in that situation. No, he made sure that his taunts were the most vicious only when the bar was crowded, when there were plenty of witnesses, everyone aware that David was on parole and didn't dare touch him.

His fingers formed a tight, hard fist as he battled the urge to give back some of what he'd been forced to take. He wanted to hurt this bully, wanted to take back his dignity, to stand tall and not back down to anyone ever again. He'd swallowed a bellyful of humiliation and shame, and some days his insides were stained black with self-loathing.

At those moments even thoughts of his mother, so

fragile and needy, were barely enough to pull him back from the edge. He forced himself to go when every fiber of him craved to stay. To avenge.

"That's right, you candy-ass coward—run. Run like the spineless murderer you are," shouted Patton.

Each word was a spike driven into his brain, a lash on his back, a barb worming its way into what remained of his self-respect.

When Patton began laughing, David truly understood what it was to hate.

He just wasn't sure who he despised more, Patton or himself.

A SMALL, NEAT WOMAN SMILED as Callie entered Albert Manning's reception area, formerly the living room, she imagined, of the frame house this building had been. The furnishings were slightly shabby, but the space carried an air of welcome she appreciated right now after the bruising encounter with David.

She felt strangely vulnerable, robbed of the dream that out there somewhere in the world was a decent, honorable teen grown into an even better man.

That couldn't matter; she was strong on her own. She didn't need anyone. She had made herself.

Finally the sweet-faced little woman looked up. "Mr. Manning can see you now." She rose and escorted Callie through the door behind her desk.

"Good morning." The older man crossed to her. "I hope you slept well." He gestured her to a chair. "Would you care for anything? Coffee? Tea?"

"No." She had to force herself to slow down, to return the courtesy. "But thank you. It was nice of you to provide food at Miss Margaret's. I'm afraid I didn't do justice to it."

"My wife will be sorry to hear that. She enjoys feeding people. Perhaps you could join us for dinner tonight instead."

"I'll be halfway to Philadelphia by dinnertime."

He studied her as if measuring her, clearly disappointed by what he found. "I suppose you'd like to get on with it, then."

"I would."

"Very well." He opened the folder in front of him. Scoured his desk for something, then felt the top of his head where reading glasses perched. He put them on, then spent time picking up pages, thumbing through them, setting them back down so slowly Callie thought she might scream.

Then he sighed. "Miss Margaret was not generally a sentimental woman, with a few exceptions. One of those—" he looked at her over the top of his glasses "—was you."

"Me?"

"My conversations with her, in drawing up this will as well as knowing her over the years, led me to believe that she considered you to be a great failure on her part." At Callie's quiet gasp, he shook his head. "I do not mean you were the failure, but rather that she considered herself to have failed you." He paused to clean his glasses on the end of his tie. "I apologize, Ms. Hunter.

Miss Margaret was an old and dear friend of mine, and something more in our youth. I confess to having a difficult time dealing with her loss."

Callie realized that his eyes were slightly reddened, and couldn't help being touched. She'd always wondered why Miss Margaret never married, and it was on the tip of her tongue to ask, except that this nice gentleman was already distressed. So she merely nodded in sympathy. "She was a special lady. But why on earth would she think she'd failed me?"

"She told me once that you reminded her of herself."

Callie blinked. "I can't begin to imagine how. Or why. Surely Miss Margaret was never a rebel." She tried to imagine the sweet older woman in Goth black and chains, spike-tipped hair. Though there had been those earrings... Callie found herself grinning.

"You have a lovely smile," he said, returning it. "Actually, you'd be wrong about that. Miss Margaret was very forward thinking for her time. If she'd been born twenty-five years later, she'd have been burning her brassiere with the rest of the feminists."

For some reason, the word *brassiere,* so old-fashioned, was surprisingly embarrassing to hear from a man who could be her grandfather. "Really?" She thought back to some of Miss Margaret's conversations and realized that she'd only looked at the older woman through the eyes of someone who'd been certain anyone over twenty-five was ancient. "Now that you mention it, she was her own woman, wasn't she?"

"Very much so. She did things her own way, always.

I believe she would have liked a family of her own, but—" His eyes grew sad again. "It wasn't meant to be." He lifted his gaze to hers. "She enjoyed her time with you very much."

"I can't see why. I was a major pain in the behind."

"You were young and vulnerable. She felt that if she had handled you better, perhaps you wouldn't have sought comfort in David Langley, and then you wouldn't have—"

Gotten pregnant, she finished silently for him. "She was kind to me, and I liked her, too, but I'm not sure there was an adult alive I would have listened to."

"When you lost the baby," he said gingerly, watching her reaction, which she carefully kept neutral, "she was devastated. It only pointed out what a poor chaperone she'd been, she believed, and your mother certainly emphasized that when she returned to take you back to South Carolina."

"My mother wasn't fit to raise kittens." Her mother had used sex as a currency, trading out boyfriends like some women changed hair color, and some of them were slimier than others. That particular one had begun trying to get Callie alone, and he wasn't the first to make her skin crawl. Her mother never put Callie first, though, and when she'd tried to speak up this time, her mother had sent her away rather than protecting her.

"Miss Margaret knew that, and she tried everything to get your mother to leave you here permanently. She even offered your mother money."

Callie's eyes popped. "I'm astonished that my

mother didn't take it. I ran away from her three months later and never went back. She could have saved herself a lot of aggravation."

"Be that as it may, Miss Margaret wanted some way to make up to you what she considered an enormous failing on her part." He adjusted his glasses and looked at her. "Which is why she made you her primary heir."

"Heir? To what? There's only her little house."

He smiled fondly. "I'm afraid there's more, Ms. Hunter. Miss Margaret lived frugally, I grant you, but she was a shrewd investor. She believed a woman should be able to take care of herself financially and should never be under a man's thumb simply because she had no resources of her own."

"I can't argue with that."

"Not that she disliked men, of course." At this, he blushed a bit, and Callie was more curious than ever. "She had her beaux. She believed in true love."

Beaux. Callie tried to imagine Miss Margaret primping for a date. She glanced up at Manning, wondering where he fit into the mix, but he quickly looked away.

He cleared his throat. "At any rate, Miss Margaret owns—owned," he corrected, "thirty-four houses in Oak Hollow that she either rented out or owner-financed. Those houses and mortgages she left to you, along with a substantial block of stocks and bonds purchased with the revenue those properties generated. She also left you her personal home."

Thirty-four houses? And stocks? Bonds? Callie, who had never owned anything but a car, was staggered. "I—I don't—what am I going to do with all that?"

"Collect the rents and payments, I suppose," he said mildly. Then he frowned. "Not all of them are current, however. Miss Margaret was a little too forgiving in her later years." Then his mouth tightened. "One mortgage, in particular, has been in arrears for nearly a year and must be dealt with." He looked up at her. "It belongs to Delia Compton."

"Who?"

"You knew her as Delia Langley."

David's mother.

"Tell me what happened to David and his mother. No more hints, no more innuendo. Lay it out for me." She hadn't wanted to dig deeper, but now she had to.

"Langley killed a man, I told you that."

"Who?"

"Ned Compton."

"Compton? His—"

Manning nodded. "His own stepfather. Ned had moved to Oak Hollow with the idea of developing this area into a tourist destination. He would have provided jobs, given this place lifeblood. People began to feel hope for the first time in memory, thanks to him."

"When did she marry him?"

"Not long after you…left." Manning squirmed. "She thought a father figure would help her get David straightened out."

Straightened out? The town's golden boy? David had jeopardized his very bright future to do the right thing once he'd found out she was pregnant. He'd stood by her against everyone when she refused to consider giving up the baby. "There was nothing wrong with David. He was the best person I ever met."

"Begging your pardon, Ms. Hunter, but you weren't here. He went bad after you left, cutting school and starting fights. He turned into someone none of us knew, though not a soul in Oak Hollow would have ever believed him capable of murder."

The David she'd known had been the soul of kindness, strong and upright and gentle. "What was the evidence against him?" She fell back on her training as she sought to understand what she was hearing.

"There was a fireplace poker with his prints on it, that and his confession. His lawyer pleaded for mercy and leaned heavily on David's former good reputation to get the charges reduced to manslaughter. Folks around here were plenty riled up about that. Ned was going to be our salvation and his killer should still be in jail, most folks think."

"But—" Callie could not believe what she was hearing, yet the hard, angry man bore no resemblance to the gentle boy.

He went bad after you left.

"Where does he live now?"

"With her. He has a job," the attorney said with distaste, "but it will not be sufficient to make a dent in the back payments."

Wait a minute. Wait—*she* held the mortgage on David's house now? "I can't—I don't—"

"There's more."

Still trying to absorb the news, she only nodded for him to go on.

"There's a condition." He waited a beat, but when she didn't respond, he continued. "Miss Margaret wanted you to live here, in her house, for at least thirty days before you are allowed use of any of the income for more than living expenses."

Thirty days? Callie was incredulous. "I live in Philadelphia. I have a job. I'm—" *I have to salvage my future there, forced leave or not.* She began to laugh. "This is absurd. Completely ridiculous." Abruptly she sobered. "What happens if I reject all of it?"

"You can't."

She stood and straightened her pencil skirt. "Of course I can."

"Ms. Hunter. Please sit down. Calm yourself."

"Calm myself? When she—" Callie was aghast at the nerve of the woman she'd been feeling sentimental over.

He held up a hand. "I didn't word that right. What I meant was that many people will suffer if you don't accept this. She left no alternative heir, so the properties would all have to be dealt with by the state of Georgia. The most likely course for the government would be to appoint an administrator who would dispose of the properties. Many of them are inhabited by families who've lived there into the second and third generation, but an outsider wouldn't care about any of that."

"You can't be serious." She sought to recollect whatever she'd learned about estate law, but she was a criminal attorney, not a civil one. Licensed in Pennsylvania, not Georgia.

"You're welcome to check out the law for yourself, Ms. Hunter, if you don't believe me." He studied her over the top of his glasses, patient and somehow too knowing. "I can certainly understand why you would have conflicted feelings about Oak Hollow, but are you honestly willing to throw all these people to the wolves just to escape dealing with the past?"

Callie stared at him.

Implacably he stared back.

Are you a coward? was what he was asking really.

Of course she wasn't. She was a busy woman with a lot on her mind.

She closed her eyes for a second. Breathed deep. There was a solution, a way out. There had to be.

I will not let this place get the best of me, not ever again.

CHAPTER FOUR

SHE DESPERATELY WANTED an Internet connection so she could find an argument to refute Albert Manning's opinion. The likelihood of high-speed Internet in Oak Hollow, though, wasn't something she'd care to bet on.

How she wished her boss hadn't ordered her to take extended time off. Her feeling of urgency to return to Philadelphia and salvage her career hadn't abated as she'd put miles between herself and the city—rather, every moment away ratcheted up her anxiety. She had absolutely no interest in fixing the mess Miss Margaret had dropped in her lap; a much more critical problem awaited her.

Callie pulled into the driveway of the house she'd been given, but any lingering sentiment from this morning had evaporated under the harsh sun of Manning's unpleasant surprise. Houses—and the people living in them—were the least of her worries.

She pressed her lips together. Including the one that put a roof over David's head.

She let her forehead sink against her fists, which were clenched on the steering wheel. If she'd known this tangle would be waiting to greet her, she'd never have come. Albert Manning, however much the essential gentleman, would have been easier to resist from eight hundred miles away. Instead, she'd agreed to begin a tour of Miss Margaret's properties this very afternoon.

The knock on her window made her jump.

A child stood there. The mouth moved and thin arms gestured, but Callie couldn't hear through the closed window. Rather than start the engine to roll down the window, Callie opened the door carefully so as not to hit the child. She couldn't decide if it was a boy or a girl.

"I did the watering."

"What?" Standing now, Callie saw that the child's head came only to her midriff.

"I watered the garden like Miss Margaret taught me." The child's frame was skinny all over and was clad in worn jeans and a shapeless, too-big T-shirt. The clothing gave Callie no clues as to gender, nor did the mop of dark brown hair that might have been bowl cut, but the delicate features seemed to belong to a girl.

"Heard Miss Margaret had someone staying here. Didn't want the plants to die even if she—" The girl's eyes cut away, but not before Callie saw grief in them. "She wouldn't like that. Anyway, food shouldn't be wasted."

"Who are you?" Callie asked.

"Jessie Lee. Chambers," the girl added. "Granny and me live on the Ridge in one of Miss Margaret's rent houses. Who are you? What are you doing here?" she challenged.

The Ridge. Where David's house was—but she wouldn't think about that now. "My name is Callie Hunter. Miss Margaret was my great-aunt."

"You taking over?" The girl's gaze darted to her. "'Cause Granny is putting together the rent money as fast as she can, and I can do some more work for you to make up the difference, just like I did for Miss Margaret."

Oh, man. Callie did not want the people in those properties to become real. "What kind of work?"

"Anything she needed. I'm strong. I can cut the grass, help can the vegetables from the garden, wash the windows. I painted the toolshed, and I was supposed to help paint the inside, but she—" Jessie Lee shrugged and didn't finish.

"How old are you?"

"Thirteen." But her gaze cut away, and Callie was fairly certain she was lying, that she was, in fact, younger.

So much came back to Callie then, how the children in these pockets of poverty had to grow up and assume responsibility at much younger ages than their suburban counterparts. Inner-city kids grew up fast, as well, but far too often learned a much different set of survival skills centered around violence, not gardening or household chores.

The fear she saw in this girl's eyes softened Callie's resentment that she was being forced to get involved. "How often did Miss Margaret employ you?"

"Depends on how Granny's money was holding out." Jessie Lee shrugged, but her expression was wary. "You gonna change everything?"

"I—" How did she answer? She settled for the truth. "I have no idea. I—I wasn't prepared for this."

"Anything you need to know, you just ask me. I can help you." The girl's words were rushed. "I know I don't look it, but I'm strong, I swear. I can manage whatever I need to."

The plea was difficult to resist. "Is your pay current?"

"Miss Margaret didn't give me money. She just kept my hours and worked it out with my granny."

Callie frowned. "Do you know where she kept the records?"

Jessie Lee tapped her temple. "In her head, best I could tell."

Oh, Miss Margaret... But the girl's worry got to Callie. She'd run away at fifteen, and she could remember the anxiety of having no security and no control only too well. She'd have to consult with Albert, as well as Jessie Lee's grandmother. In the meantime, though, she could put a little power back into the girl's hands. "How about this? You make me a list of what you've done for the last month, best you can recall, while I'm sorting things out."

"I could do that," the girl replied eagerly.

"I'm not ready to think about painting inside the house, but perhaps you could continue to care for the garden until I get things figured out."

"Yes, ma'am. Grass needs cutting, too."

Callie had her doubts about the child's ability to handle a mower, but she was all too aware of how desperation could lend strength. "Then let's go look at the mower."

"Yes, ma'am!" Jessie Lee's worry lines disappeared, and for the moment at least, Callie had a small sense of making progress.

Plus a welcome distraction from the afternoon's tour.

Which would include the house where David was living.

IT WAS TOO BLASTED HOT to be running, but David had learned in prison that wearing yourself out exercising could drain some of the fury when locking it down was beyond him. Sometimes no amount of logic or self-discipline could help.

Walking away from the earlier confrontation would only increase Mickey Patton's contempt, but David had forced himself to do it anyway. He would never risk being put behind bars again, so he'd run up one hill and down the other, so many miles that he knew he'd be rubber-legged when he stopped. After he finally retrieved his mother's sedan and drove home, all he could think about was a long shower, some food and a nap before work.

When he spotted Albert Manning's car out front, he got a sinking feeling. His mother was behind on her house payments, and Manning handled Miss Margaret's affairs.

This couldn't be good.

David crossed to the back steps, sweaty and filthy from his run and the dust on the roads he'd traveled. He followed the sound of the voices before realizing there was a third one.

He stopped dead at the entrance to the hallway as Callie Hunter stepped out of his bedroom.

His *bedroom*. The one place in this world—the only space for fifteen endless years—where he had the right to close the door. To shut out everything and everyone.

Callie wasn't alone, either; his mother and Manning were with her. The feeling of violation was so intense that he gripped the door frame before he could leap into action. Before he said something that couldn't be taken back.

He had almost nothing in this life that belonged to him anymore—not his good name or control over his future, barely the clothes on his body—but that one miserable, small room was the place he'd begun to relax, just a little. To quit feeling hunted by fate and choices made, by a world that had rendered a verdict and found him wanting. It wasn't home—no place was now—but it was still a refuge. His mother honored his unspoken need for privacy, for a spot where he didn't have to worry about fighting for his life or hurting the innocent, and he'd started counting on that.

Now strangers were breaching it, and it didn't matter that one of them had been a girl he'd cared about, had stupidly tried to shield.

The woman before him was not that girl. The man behind her represented the system and the town that had turned their backs on him long ago.

"Get out."

"David!" his mother gasped.

"You have no business here," said the lawyer. "This is between your mother and Ms. Hunter. She now owns the mortgage."

David's gaze snapped to Callie's. He could see nothing of the young girl who'd cried in his arms. The woman who stared back was a stranger.

With the upper hand.

"Tables are turned now. Feel good?" he asked Callie.

"Here, now," the lawyer said. "You've got no call to talk to her like that."

"I can speak for myself," Callie said coolly.

Her expression revealed that she'd indeed heard all about him, not that it was any surprise. Plenty of people would be happy to fill her ears with the salacious story.

His mother's face was white with strain and horror, but David was beyond social niceties. "You can't want to be here. Not in Oak Hollow."

Callie's flinch was barely visible, but something flickered in her eyes before she looked away. "I have business to attend to."

He had to reach past the polished woman to the girl who might remember what he'd given up for her. "Don't do this, Callie." His mother would never survive losing her home. However desperately he wanted away from Oak Hollow, that was too high a price to pay for his freedom.

"You are in no position to make demands." The lawyer stepped forward. "You need to leave now. Haven't you done enough to your mother?"

"I'm talking to Callie, not you." David didn't budge. "Are you afraid to face me?"

"I'm not afraid of anything." At last she looked at him, and her chin jutted.

The moment pulsated with too many memories, too much that could never be said.

"Please," his mother said to Callie. "He doesn't mean offense."

Her pleading tone grated on him, but her genuine fear was palpable. If he pushed too hard, in a matter of days, weeks at most, the lawyer and Callie could have his mother out on the street, with no place to go. All of them knew that.

"Forget it," he said, even though everything in him wanted to fight the threat they presented.

But the lawyer was right. He was in no position to demand anything.

He turned on his heel and walked away.

THE AIR, poisoned by the cloud of his fury, was too thick to breathe.

"Being back here is hard for him," David's mother defended.

Callie could relate. She wanted to be in Philly, not touring these properties, but Albert had insisted, intent on bringing these people alive for her so that she couldn't easily walk away from her inheritance.

In reality she didn't want to walk, she wanted to run. Faster even than David had disappeared, she longed to put distance between herself and this place, between past and present.

She'd worked hard to grow beyond the troubled teen, to prove herself worthy and to be a success. She hadn't planned on the case of a lifetime coming her way or a bad break pushing her into a gamble that now jeopardized the very foundation of the life she'd made.

But the pale, thin woman before her was not at fault. "We'll figure something out, Mrs. Langley," she said.

"Compton," Albert prompted.

"Langley," David's mother argued, raising Albert's eyebrows with the unexpected vehemence. "David is trying, you have to understand. I let things get out of hand when he was—when he was away." She shifted her gaze back to Callie, eyes pleading. "He's a good man. You know who he really is."

Do I? Callie wondered. She tried to square the boy she'd known with the hard, angry man she'd encountered this time around. She knew what prison did to people—hadn't she seen the revolving door often enough? To survive inside those walls required turning your back on every scrap of humanity you possessed.

Delia Langley gripped her forearm. "Please. He's doing all he can to get us back on solid footing. He only needs a little more time."

"Mrs. Langley…" *I can't do this. I don't want the responsibility.* Walking through the monk's cell that was David's room, the sense of wrongness, of trespassing had rolled through her stomach in greasy waves.

What did missed payments matter to her when she would return to her life and her salary and her small but hardly used apartment? They counted for much more to a woman who'd lost two husbands and, for all intents and purposes, a son she had adored. How could Callie tear Jessie Lee's world apart, or this woman's, or any of their neighbors'? Life here was too hard without being tossed from their homes by some bureaucrat or number-cruncher.

She didn't want to stay for Miss Margaret's thirty days, but she would remain here long enough to craft a solution, and legally break her great-aunt's provision, and then she would be able to leave Oak Hollow and her memories behind, perhaps even put them to rest.

"You won't lose your home. Miss Margaret wouldn't have wanted that."

The relief that rose brought a little color back into the woman's cheeks. "She was always very kind to me, to a lot of folks."

"I know. I was one of them." This was the closest she had ever come to a discussion of the past with the woman who'd despised Callie for luring her golden son into his downfall, dressing like a siren and acting much older than she was. David, though compassionate and mature, was also a teenage boy with all the attendant hormones, and Callie, with only her mother as an example of how to treat men, had taken advantage. "I'll see what can be done to give him more time to come up with the money."

"Thank you," the woman murmured. "Thank you so much."

Callie led her to a rocker with soft, worn cushions shaped to fit the woman's thin frame. She stayed longer than she wanted to, making sure David's mother was calmer before she felt it was all right to leave.

Once they'd left, however, she turned on Albert Manning and that satisfied smile on his face. She didn't want this, any of it. Looking back never accomplished anything, only moving forward counted.

She lifted her chin. "Let's get finished. Where to next?"

If the older man looked startled, maybe disapproving, well, it meant nothing to her. Life wasn't a popularity contest. She would take care of what she had to and move on.

CHAPTER FIVE

SHE COULDN'T SETTLE.

After an endless day touring properties, the sight of all those anxious faces lingered. Exhausted as Callie was, she couldn't seem to relax. She had washed the meager store of clothes she'd bought to tide her over until her assistant Anna could send her own things. Now she paced Miss Margaret's house, flipped the television channels without seeing, picked up three different books from the shelves and none of them snagged her attention. She wasn't hungry, and try as she might to focus on her career, not a single plan to rescue it would form.

She slapped open the screen door and walked outside. Down the front walk and out onto the road she strode, hoping exercise would take the edge off the restlessness that would not leave her alone.

It wasn't until a couple of miles later when she spotted the cemetery off to the left that she realized where she'd been heading without thinking.

She'd have a word with Miss Margaret.

And, if she could summon the courage, she'd visit that small grave she'd been running from for years.

She entered between the columns of stacked stones that had been there for generations. Miss Margaret's plot was easy to find—a high mound of fresh dirt covered with wilting blossoms. As Callie approached, she thought about how much had changed in only two days since she'd last stood here.

"You have some nerve," she began. "What do you expect me to do? This is crazy. I don't belong here. You can't possibly think—" Her shoulders sank on a sigh. She couldn't seem to sustain her fury after all, and a wry smile wouldn't be stifled. "I loved you, you know. I have no idea what you saw in me—" Callie was shocked at the choking rush of emotion. She'd never understood why Miss Margaret would go to so much trouble for her. They were the most unlikely of companions, yet now, years later, Callie realized that in many ways, Miss Margaret was the best friend she'd ever had.

She'd loved Callie, too, even though tender words hadn't come easily to her.

"You lived your words instead, didn't you?" She'd taught by example, and a powerful one it had been. Margaret Jennings might have borne no children and married no man, but in her own fashion, she'd nurtured a town nonetheless.

"I'm not like you," Callie murmured. "I can't—"

Can't or won't? she could almost hear Miss Margaret challenge, just as she had so often, over big things or small. *Can't sew? Here, fix this button, hem these pants. Can't cook? Knead this dough and next thing you know, you've got bread.*

Can't go back to school and finish? How do you plan to keep this baby if you can't feed it? Don't you dare expect that boy to take care of you both.

Miss Margaret had no use for the word *can't,* and no patience for *won't.*

After Callie's mother had dragged her back to South Carolina once she'd lost the baby, she'd run away, yet Miss Margaret's voice had followed her. *Be practical, child. A woman's got to take care of herself, and you can't do that without that diploma.*

For all that Callie had neglected Miss Margaret for so many years, she realized now that she'd carried the older woman with her as she'd worked her way into community college, then university and, at last, law school. Callie's mother had understood *can't* all too well—her whole life had been spent depending on one sleazy man after another rather than taking care of herself. If the search for a way for the world to make sense had driven Callie to law school, it was Miss Margaret who'd made her stay and finish.

Yet Callie had still let Miss Margaret go. She'd never been the type to navel gaze; introspection got in the way of accomplishment. Looking back at the most painful period of her life would have hamstrung her, would have anchored her in the land of regrets.

But she'd never even said thank-you, and admitting it now nearly brought her to her knees. How could she have neglected Miss Margaret all these years?

Her mind darted in search of a solution, some way to undo this grievous wrong. Her focus landed on the spot where a headstone would stand, and she vowed that it would be a special one that she would provide herself.

Still, it was not nearly the legacy Miss Margaret deserved.

In that moment, what Miss Margaret was asking of her with her bequest struck Callie with force. *Take care of my people,* she could almost hear her asking. That was a legacy that would appeal to the woman who'd quietly given so much to so many.

Including Callie herself.

A woman is as strong as a man any day, Miss Margaret had told her often, *we just don't beat our chests or flex our muscles to show it.*

How, then? a skeptical Callie had asked.

We endure, Callie Anne. We are the backbone.

Backbone. Callie had been known for being tough on crime, for being ruthless, but she'd taken a shortcut in Philly rather than risk losing her high-profile case.

She'd had almost three weeks after the end of the trial to stew over her failure, then to worry about complications when the defense counsel had gotten wind of a conversation Callie had had with the sister of one of the witnesses for the prosecution. The sister had told Callie that the witness had an axe to grind with the defendant who, she claimed, had raped and beaten her and gotten away with it. Whether or not that was the case crucial evidence had already been excluded from the trial because of procedural errors made by the police, and Callie badly needed the witness's testimony to connect the defendant and the murder victim.

So Callie hadn't told anyone. Had let the woman testify. In the end, Callie's ethical lapse hadn't affected the outcome of the trial—the defendant had gone free—but the D.A. had found out what she'd done, and she'd had to face both him and her own conscience, that she'd been so desperate to win that she'd started down a very slippery slope.

That was when, out of the blue, the news about Miss Margaret's death had come. Now she was being forced to deal with her past…and all these people and their problems she felt unequal to solving.

How could she do that when she wasn't even sure she could solve her own?

She lifted her head and looked across the grass. She'd never faced the child whose death she still believed, in her heart of hearts, was her fault, no matter that the midwife had assured her that these things just happened.

Callie couldn't stay in Oak Hollow, that much was true, but wasn't there some way to do right by the people who'd depended on Miss Margaret without miring herself here? "I'll figure something out, Miss Margaret. I won't let you down."

Then Callie straightened and took the first step toward living up to that promise. As the shadows lengthened, she made her way across the grass.

She saw the angel first.

No cherub, nothing soft or sweet or cloying—this sculpture evoked the fierceness in the word *guardian*. First curious, then entranced, Callie was drawn to the marker for its very difference from everything around it. Not until she stood a few feet away did she realize that it was not made of stone but wood turned silver by the force of the elements.

She knelt and reached out to touch it, but before she could, the stone lying flat on the ground caught her.

Froze her.

Hunter Langley, she read.

Callie rocked back on her heels, struck to the heart. Hunter…Langley. She'd been too dazed to name the child who'd never drawn breath. Who…?

Her attention rose to the angel, and she knew.

David had done this. He'd had a gift with wood, but never had she seen anything he'd carved to match the powerful beauty of this.

When, though? The marker must have been here for some time, and David was only recently out of prison. He'd been a mere boy when all this happened, still open and trusting. Able to hurt, to grieve.

To name their baby for both of them. *Oh, David…* She mourned that boy along with their child.

Was there a scrap of him left in the man who'd wished her to hell as she'd breached his privacy a few hours earlier?

At last, she let herself touch the wood, the pads of her fingers gliding over the silken curves. How could the hands that had created this—for she had no doubt at all that his had—also take the life of another man? She couldn't square the two.

He turned into someone none of us knew.

Had they all romanticized him? she wondered now.

She'd been fourteen when they met. Had she made him into a hero because she'd needed him to be? The prosecutor in her had learned hard lessons about reality.

He definitely wasn't that hero now. Maybe he never had been. There was no question, however, that she'd torn through his life like a cyclone.

After you...left.

How much of the blame for David's fate rested squarely with her?

SHORTHANDED TONIGHT, the bar's owner, Carl Hodges, had asked David to come in early to bus tables and help out in front. The bar was crowded, and the mood was ugly. People were worried and muttering about what would happen to them now that the Yankee had a knife to their throats. How would they live, *where* would they live, if she demanded that they catch up on the missed payments? Life was hard in these parts; most people were just getting by. Folks were scared, and scared made a person mean.

Mickey Patton, who'd fancied himself Ned Compton's bosom buddy when in reality he'd been Ned's tool, needed only to breathe to be mean. He'd been hurling insults at David since the moment he'd walked in tonight, obviously itching to force another confrontation.

David would relish nothing more than to oblige, but Mickey Patton didn't have a criminal record to slow his fists down. David gave the man wide berth, however much that stuck in his craw.

"Hey, boy!" Patton slammed his beer bottle down on the table late into the night. "Another round over here. 'Less you've got a crapper you oughta be cleaning." He laughed uproariously, and his two dim-witted buddies joined in.

David glanced over at Carl, but he was occupied. "Get it yourself." Most people did as a rule. The bar was nothing fancy, and Carl hired no waitresses.

"I'm sitting here at Ned's table, you murdering son of a bitch, and you—"

David moved away. Closed his ears and let their taunts slide right off. Busied himself filling a tray with empties and headed to the kitchen. There he set the tray down with a thud and grabbed a trash bag to carry out to the Dumpster out back. He needed this job, but if he didn't get his head clear, something bad was going to happen. He was still simmering over the afternoon's humiliation, and he shared the same worry others were voicing.

What would she do, this Callie he barely recognized? She hated Oak Hollow and everything it stood for. He couldn't really blame her—the way she'd been treated back then had been shameful.

And then there'd been the heartache.

He was nearly to the Dumpster when he heard the door slam against the wall. He whirled to see Patton with a gleam of metal in his hand and two of his drink-ing buddies by his side.

"I have just about had enough of you, boy."

CHAPTER SIX

THE SUN STREAMED through a gap in the pale cream curtains. Callie awoke and stretched, surveying Miss Margaret's bedroom. *Her* bedroom now, she reminded herself, though it couldn't look less like her barely decorated apartment in the city. She only slept there; most of her waking hours were spent at work.

An oval rag rug in shades of rose and green covered golden oak flooring. A maple vanity with a big round mirror sat on the wall to her left. A matching chest, its glow soft with the patina of time and much polishing, stood opposite the cedar hope chest at the foot of the double bed where Callie snuggled beneath the log cabin quilt Miss Margaret had been piecing back when Callie lived with her.

The breeze from the open corner windows still held the cool of morning, and for the first time she could remember, Callie had nowhere to be, no jam-packed schedule waiting. She was tempted to roll over and fall back asleep.

Until she heard the singing.

She sat up and parted the curtains. In the garden,

Jessie Lee held a hose while she sang in a high, sweet voice. The tune sounded slightly familiar, but Callie couldn't place it immediately.

Then she realized where she'd heard it. A hymn, an old one she'd first listened to when Miss Margaret had dragged her to church. Callie's mother would never have darkened the door of such an establishment, so Callie's religious education had been lacking even the basics. She'd gone under protest and only because Miss Margaret wouldn't hear otherwise. Callie hadn't cared much for the curious glances, especially as her belly grew ever rounder, but attendance, she'd figured, was the price she had to pay to stay near David. He'd been there, too, moving from his mother's side to stand as a sentinel beside Callie, a bulwark against the muttering.

Callie hadn't listened a lot to the sermons or paid much attention to the scriptures, but she'd been transported by the music. Miss Margaret's church had no piano or organ; everything was sung a cappella, the congregation dividing into harmonies automatically. Somehow, on those Sundays, all her fears and worries had taken second place as the music of old-time gospel hymns wrapped themselves around Callie's anxious heart and soothed her like a soft, warm blanket. They'd lifted her spirits and made her feel a little hope that maybe she wouldn't be the world's worst mama, that perhaps everyone was wrong and she and David could overcome the odds against them.

Those bits of hope had shattered on that night Callie never let herself think about. She ran one hand over her flat stomach now, felt the lean body she'd fashioned through daily workouts. Impossible to believe that once this belly had been filled with a growing new life. That her childish dreams of a fantasy family had actually seemed possible.

Being here made her remember that once she'd been vulnerable. The years since had been devoted to making herself tough. Invincible. Lady Justice.

She'd been bruised by recent events, but she wouldn't stay that way. Who knew better than she that dreams could be blasted to bits?

She lived in the real, in the harsh, cold truth. In the city where the strong survived and the weak suffered.

She was not weak—hadn't she proved that time and again? Callie shoved the covers back and stood. She couldn't get caught up in sunlight and sweet singing. She had research to do, plans to make, an escape route to plot out. Still shaken by what she'd seen yesterday of the lives that were now in her hands, she resolved to find a solution that would allow her to leave in good conscience.

Number one on the list was Jessie Lee's pay; number two was David's house and all the others like it.

At the thought of David, she remembered the angel on the tiny grave. Did he carve anymore? Was anything of that gifted artisan still inside him? She wondered if she'd ever know the answer. Moving across the floor barefoot, she headed for the kitchen and coffeepot first, then a shower.

A knock on the door interrupted her as she was

scooping grounds. "Callie—Ms. Hunter. Please open the door." A woman's voice. Frantic.

Was that—? Callie frowned. It couldn't be David's mother.

"Please—you have to help me!"

Callie rushed into the living room and answered the summons.

It was indeed Delia Langley, looking, if anything, worse than the day before. "Oh, thank heavens! You have to help me." She grasped at Callie's hand. "You have to come."

"What is it? What's wrong?" Callie drew her inside. David's mother was shaking, her eyes darting around, desperation and fear in every line of her frame.

"It's David. We have to go." Delia yanked at Callie's hand as if she'd drag her bodily through the door.

"Calm down. Tell me what's happened."

"He's—they called me just now. Oh, God—he's in jail. They've arrested him. I can't—it's happening all over again." She twisted her hands in fretful circles.

"Arrested? For what?"

"Mickey Patton—he's been badly beaten. They're saying it was David, but he wouldn't have. He—you have to help him."

"I'm a prosecutor, not a defense attorney. There's nothing I can do."

"You have to." David's mother grabbed Callie. "No one else will. He didn't do this, I'm telling you."

Callie only stared at her. "I can't help him."

"Please…" Delia's eyes were wild now, and she

swayed on her feet so badly Callie had to steady her. "You're his only hope. Do whatever you want with my house, put me out on the streets, but please, just go see him. Make them let him out of there. He'll go crazy being locked up again." With effort, Delia Langley gathered herself, her eyes boring into Callie. "You owe him. He stood by you, and he paid a bigger price than you can imagine. If you care anything at all about justice, stand by him now."

Every protest dried in Callie's throat as she took in the cold, hard truth. David had stood by her when everyone they knew pushed her to give the baby up for adoption. He was already working part time, had always made straight As while playing quarterback for the football team. But soon his grades began to slip and his athletic performance suffered. Callie had not one friend in town besides him and Miss Margaret so she'd been clingy and was often sick. When the baby was stillborn she'd been mired in her own suffering and failed to see that he'd been suffering, too.

His mother was on the mark. Callie had turned her back on David, assuming he'd come out on top as he always had. Whoever David Langley was now, she realized she owed a debt to the boy he'd been, one that was long overdue.

"I'm not licensed in Georgia. There's not much I can do legally." She held up a hand as the protest formed. "But I will go see him because you're right—I do owe him. Just don't get your hopes up." She didn't envy this woman the choice she faced, trying to help the son who'd murdered her husband, but Callie's job had taught her that the world was never black or white. Her son was all Delia Langley had left. Maybe that wiped away some of his guilt or maybe children had a hold on the heart that transcended any other actions—Callie had no idea what Delia was thinking.

The reality was that she could do little, and the bitter man she'd encountered was probably guilty anyway.

But she had her own burden of guilt for whatever part she'd played in his fate. She could do this one thing and erase some of it. "All right," she said. "Let me get dressed, and I'll go with you."

Delia shook her head. "He won't see me. I've tried."

Callie frowned. "How do you know he'll see me, then?"

Weary eyes hardened. "You'll have to manage."

Great. "I can't promise anything, but I'll call you when I'm finished." After Delia left, Callie leaned back against the door, staring into the empty distance.

Then she roused herself and went to dress.

HE'D BEEN TAKEN all the way to the county seat forty miles northeast, population fourteen thousand. The county jail was small and unaccustomed to housing hardened criminals.

Getting in required some fancy talking, but Callie persuaded people for a living. She'd thought a simple reminder about the perils of questioning a prisoner who wanted legal counsel would do the trick, but she hadn't counted on a pro bono attorney already having been appointed. Apparently the local judge was on his toes.

Callie got the lawyer's name and nearly left then. David wasn't alone in this, after all; she could go in good conscience.

Halfway to the door, she remembered the angel. Maybe David didn't need an attorney, but a familiar face might be welcome, even if it was hers. Anyway, she had some questions to ask him—or some appreciation to extend, at the very least.

She retraced her steps and requested to meet with the prisoner, then held her breath. At last, the deputy on duty reluctantly agreed to go get his newest inmate.

IN PRISON, at least you had a space to retreat to. No real privacy, but the back and side walls of your cell were solid. No such luck here.

"Heard you killed somebody," said one of the inmates in the general holding cell next to him.

David, as an ex-con and convicted murderer, had been put in his own separate cage, no doubt for the sake of the petty criminals, all three of them.

"You don't look so good," said a second man.

David sought the invisible shield every prison inmate quickly acquired. He said nothing, partly because his ribs hurt too much to speak unnecessarily.

Inside, David was hanging on by his fingernails. *I can't be locked again. Can't do it.*

"Man don't want conversation," observed the third. "Murderer too good for us burglars and drunks, I guess."

He closed his eyes and breathed deep—until his ribs kicked up a ruckus. *Shallow breaths, remember.* The pain had one benefit—it distracted him. Forming a clear thought was hard.

Except one. *It's happening again.*

"Langley," interrupted the deputy who'd come for him last time, when his so-called lawyer had shown up. "Got a visitor."

Not his mother, surely. He'd used his one phone call to tell her to stay away. Finding him like this might finish her off. He would have to see her eventually, but not beaten and bloody. And not in cuffs, if he could help it.

He almost laughed at that. What in sweet hell had he been able to control in the past fifteen years? Once he'd confessed to killing Ned Compton, his life had been over.

"Langley, come on."

"Who is it?"

"Good-looking woman, says she's your friend."

Hoots from next door greeted the news. "Hot damn, Killer's got a woman come to visit!"

He shot them a look that shut them up. Could it be Callie? No other woman in Oak Hollow would come within a mile of him, except a couple of skanks at the bar who were titillated by the notion of getting it on with a murderer. He didn't think they'd drive an hour through the mountains for him, though.

He started to refuse, but then he remembered that Callie Hunter held the power to render his mother homeless. If he was going back to jail, he couldn't leave his mother defenseless.

God, he hurt. He wanted to lie down and sleep. To forget. To be left alone just for a little while before he had to descend into hell again. He didn't kid himself that he wasn't going back to prison.

Instead, he rose unsteadily, like an old man. Holding his ribs, he walked slowly to the door and extended his hands through the opening provided for cuffing him.

Then he shuffled along down the hall to the dingy, cramped visiting room to see a woman he'd just as soon never lay eyes on again.

HOW MANY TIMES had she been in a room like this? Callie glanced around the concrete block walls with paint peeling in splotches and felt naked without her briefcase or a proper set of files. Her trim black suit had helped bolster the image of a high-powered attorney, and she would build on that to handle this surreal situation.

The sound of the door opening had her turning.

Then she gasped and whipped her gaze to the deputy. "Has he had medical attention?"

"We're waiting on the doc," the man said, abashed. "Prisoners don't get priority, I'm afraid."

"He should be in the emergency room. This is a violation of his civil rights." She could not believe these words were coming out of her mouth—she'd derided defense attorneys often for the phrase that so easily raised her hackles.

"We've had a paramedic look him over. The hospital isn't set up to provide the security needed for dangerous prisoners."

Callie glanced at David. His face was stony, his eyes staring at the wall.

"This is inexcusable." It was. Stoic or not, David was clearly in pain. "We can file a suit on the county for this mistreatment."

"There's only four docs over at the clinic, see, and they stay real busy. One of them will be here soon. He's in no danger."

"Has his attorney been to see him?"

"Yes."

Right then, Callie made up her mind to meet the man and check him out.

"Leave it," David said, jaw tight. Color stained his cheeks.

Callie forced herself to chill out. Getting on the wrong side of the deputy would only rebound on David. "I appreciate whatever you can manage, Deputy," she said as warmly as she could.

"I can give you thirty minutes, ma'am," he said.

"Thank you."

He hesitated. "You sure about this?" His suspicious glance at David was telling.

"I'll be fine."

"I'll be right outside."

She counted to three, seeking patience. "Thank you." When the man finally left, the silence in the room was a living presence.

As was David's resentment.

"He thinks I should be afraid of you," she said, for lack of a better opening.

"You should." David still didn't look at her.

She walked closer. "How badly are you hurt?"

"I'm okay." His pallor said otherwise, as did how stiffly he held himself.

Obviously it was up to her to generate conversation. She decided to go for shock value. "Why, David?"

One quick glance. "Why what?"

She had so many questions, too many for thirty minutes. For this cramped room. "You're not stupid. I have to believe there's more to the story. I don't buy that you would try to kill another man when you just got out of prison."

A muscle jumped in his jaw. "It's none of your business."

"Your mother thinks otherwise. She was banging on my door first thing this morning, begging me to help you."

"I don't need your help."

"I beg to differ." She scanned him carefully. "Whoever this attorney is, he's not doing his job."

"Not much for him to do. They've got me convicted already."

"Then you need a better lawyer."

At last he looked at her. "You volunteering?"

Their eyes locked, and for a second, she could barely breathe for the memories that flooded her, all the ways those green eyes had looked at her in the past. "I'm not licensed in this state."

He visibly withdrew. "Doesn't matter. My guilt's a foregone conclusion."

There was fury writhing beneath the surface resignation, she could feel it. "Your mother is convinced you're innocent."

A mocking smile. "Do I look innocent?"

"You look beaten half to death. David…" She approached him then.

He sidestepped her, making his distaste clear.

Fine. They'd been at cross-purposes since the moment she'd come back.

But she didn't understand why, and she needed to. A wooden angel wouldn't leave her mind.

You owe him.

She tried again. "David, I didn't handle all of it well when—" she swallowed "—when our baby died."

Pain chased over his features, but quickly he mastered it. "Just go away, Callie. I don't need you."

That stung. Even though it might be true. "Your mother does."

He tensed more, if such a thing was possible. He faced her, though his reluctance was visible. "Don't take her house. Please." The appeal seemed dragged from deep within. "She's done nothing to deserve this. I can't—" He closed his eyes briefly. "I can't pay you now, but I'll have another job in prison. I won't earn much, but I'll send you everything I make."

This was excruciating for both of them. "Don't, David. You don't have to—" *Beg.* It was awful to see him reduced to this. "I won't put her out of her house. I promise."

She saw the relief settle over him.

"Thank you," he said quietly.

"But she's worried about you. And frankly, so am I."

His back went ramrod stiff again. "I can take care of myself."

"What happened last night?" Something was off, she could feel it.

"Just a fight."

"From what I gather, the other guy wasn't alone. Who is this Mickey Patton to you?"

"No one."

She waited, but nothing else was forthcoming. "I'm going to check into this."

His head whipped around, his green eyes hard. "Don't check. Don't do anything. Stay the hell out of my life."

"You can't stop me. I want to help you, David." It was a way to make amends for the past.

"You can't." He walked to the door and banged on it with his bound hands. "I'm done here," he said when the door opened.

CHAPTER SEVEN

THE COURT-APPOINTED ATTORNEY, Randy Capwell, was still wet behind the ears. Callie had reserved judgment until meeting him, had even waited to question his handling of David's injuries, not wanting to start out on the wrong foot.

She wasn't impressed.

Oh, he was pleasant enough and meant well, she thought as she sat in the chair he'd hastily cleared of a toppling stack of files. Not that any of this was her business, according to David.

If she had any sense, she'd listen to him. He'd killed a man, after all. Clearly he still seethed beneath his skin. Usually, she wouldn't have given a second thought to putting someone with David's history back in prison, knowing society was safer with him locked up.

But there was that angel.

"Who is your investigator?" she asked.

"I don't have one. Yet," he hastily added.

"But you will? Who do you normally use?"

She listened as he fumbled over a list of names, but she wasn't buying. "Have you filed any motions yet?"

"Ms. Hunter, I just got the case."

"But motions for discovery are standard. In David's case, a motion to suppress anything related to his prior conviction has to be top of the list, as well. Change of venue, based on his situation, is also advisable, don't you agree?"

A small frown. "Of course." But his expression told her he didn't know why seeking to keep the people of Oak Hollow off the jury was critical.

She'd listened to him a little while longer, tried to restrain the worst of the ruthlessness her concern for David provoked. It was obvious, however, that Capwell knew only what she did thus far, that the intricacies of David's situation were completely unknown to him and that he was severely overworked, as many public defenders were.

He intended to do his best, she believed that, but he was not the representation David needed. Still, he was a potential source of information, so she eased up on him.

"Thank you for seeing me when you're so busy."

"I'm happy to," he said with typical Southern hospitality. "I will know his case very soon, I promise." He glanced apologetically at the files stacked all around his tiny office.

"My first office at the D.A.'s wasn't any bigger, and our caseloads can get overwhelming. I understand." She did, but it was hard to ignore the gnawing in her belly over what he could realistically do for David, given the resources at hand.

One thing that she did learn was that he had called the jail, but David had refused to see him.

Are you crazy? As she left the meeting, she was tempted to go back to the jail and ask David what he was thinking. Maybe he was one of those prisoners who didn't know how to function in the outside world, who would commit a new crime soon after being released because the real world was too scary. Hellish or not, prison routine was familiar and if you kept your head down, didn't cross the wrong people, you could survive. You'd have three squares a day and a roof over your head, courtesy of the state.

The boy Callie had known had possessed powerful ambitions, would have found such a life anathema.

But, as she'd realized many times since returning, that boy was not this David.

"ARE YOU GOING to get him out of there?" Jessie Lee demanded that evening as she watered the garden and Callie took a stab at weeding, kneeling on the ground in her new too-stiff jeans.

"What?"

"David. Miss Margaret told me you're a lawyer. You can fix this."

The child's blithe assurance took her aback. "I'm not—I don't do that kind of work. I can't legally represent him." She faltered. The girl didn't understand the nuances of the situation.

"People are awful to him, and that's not right." The girl's riot of curls bounced with her indignation.

"It's complicated."

"I know he's been in jail before." Guileless blue eyes

watched her. "But he's always nice to me, and he helps Granny lots of times, but he won't let her tell anyone."

Curiouser and curiouser. "Helps her how?"

"He fixes things at our house, and he won't ever let her pay him. About all he'll accept is a meal now and then. He drives her to bingo when her knee is acting up. Picks up groceries for us, too."

Callie mulled over the inconsistencies.

"Miss Margaret would want you to help him."

"Why?" She'd been thinking the same, but she wanted to hear the girl's reasoning.

"He did stuff for her, too. And she always told me everybody deserves a second chance." Earnest eyes watched hers. "Don't you believe that?"

Had she once? Callie could barely remember that naive girl, after years of contact with society's dregs. "It's not that simple." When Jessie Lee's chin jutted, Callie tamped down her impatience. "Sometimes people get on a path that— They take a wrong step and—" Normally so smooth at arguing before a jury, she couldn't seem to find her rhythm.

This jury wasn't buying her case. "Who will help him if you don't?"

He doesn't want my help, Callie started to protest. *Everyone is sure he's guilty.* Her visit with the sheriff earlier that day had been more dismaying than the one with David's lawyer. The lost promise of Ned Compton's plans for Oak Hollow was still etched into the minds of its citizens.

She couldn't believe a child was calling her out. She'd

been so zealous in her search for the truth once, so
positive it could be found…when had she quit looking?
When had she ever relied on the opinions of others?

Had she lost all her courage at the end of her ill-
fated case?

Something didn't fit here. First, a wooden angel,
then this story of good deeds kept secret. Both were
more like the David she'd once known than the villain
people whispered about. The stony, silent man who
trusted no one.

"All right," Callie said. When Jessie Lee's head rose
abruptly, Callie held up a hand. "I still can't take action
on his behalf, not without associated counsel, and—"
Whatever she might have said was cut off by a skinny
little body crashing into hers.

"You can do it, I know you can. Thank you."

Callie tried to think when she'd last been hugged by
anyone not angling for sex. Awkwardly she patted the
girl's back. "I might not be able to do anything—oof!"
Thin arms squeezed more tightly, and Callie gave up the
battle, joining the embrace for a precious second until
Jessie Lee danced back.

"I'll go tell Granny!"

"Jessie Lee—" But the girl was already halfway to
the road.

Callie watched her go, wondering what she'd just
gotten herself into.

DAVID DIDN'T BELIEVE the guard the next day when the
man informed him that Callie had returned. He opened

his mouth to refuse the visit, but at the last instant, he changed his mind.

Time dragged here. He didn't have to answer her questions, and he damn sure didn't want her interfering, but she might have news about his mother's house.

God knows how he'd make payments to Callie and still send his mother money on an inmate's pay, but being sure his mother had a roof over her head would make returning to prison a little easier. That he would was a foregone conclusion; he didn't kid himself otherwise. Capwell kept mixing up his name, and the sheriff, a friend of Ned Compton's, had his mind made up about David's guilt.

A powerful urge to sink back on his bunk and give up dragged at him. What was the use of trying when he was doomed from the start?

He'd stepped on the road to failure the first day he'd laid eyes on Callie Hunter; he just hadn't known it then. Having idolized his father, David hadn't been able to walk away from his own child, however scared he was about what it meant to his plans for college and beyond. He'd done what he'd believed was right in sticking up for Callie, but he'd been out of his depth, trying to help her get over losing the baby, hadn't even known how to handle it himself. Would he ever stop hearing her animal cries of pain, seeing the blood, so much of it…feeling her small hands squeezing his much-bigger ones hard enough to rub bone against bone as she fought to deliver the baby that was coming too soon? The baby that would never breathe?

Grief had tangled with the guilt of being relieved not to have to figure out how to be a father when he was only a kid himself. Then Callie's mom had spirited her back to South Carolina, and he'd had to swallow the bitter pill of a bright future sacrificed…for what? Callie was gone, and it was like waking up from a bad dream to find an even worse reality.

Meanwhile his mother had begun seeing Ned Compton, and everything went further south after that.

"You coming or not?" the deputy asked.

What's the point, Callie? But he rose anyway, and stuck his hands through the bars, grinding his teeth against the feel of metal being snapped around his wrists.

Bound like an animal, every step watched. God, he'd thought this hell was over, that he could just move quietly through the world, keep to himself and everybody else would leave him be.

If not for Mickey Patton—

His gut clenched with the fury that never seemed to leave him. He could forget for only brief, precious moments, in the mindlessness of running or when the sun warmed his back as he tended the garden…welcome sailing on the smooth waters of life others took for granted.

"Here." The guard grabbed his elbow, yanked him into the room in front of Callie.

Just because he could.

David squeezed his eyes shut against the stabbing ache of his ribs, wished he could keep them shut long enough that Callie would disappear and not witness his debasement.

Lock it down. Ruthlessly he squelched the anger and shame, holding out his hands for the cuffs to be removed.

"Don't think so," the guard said. "Might make the lady nervous, being with a murderer."

"The lady," said Callie in a voice tinged with its own anger, "isn't one bit worried. Take them off."

"Ma'am, I don't—"

"I'll be representing Mr. Langley as co-counsel. We have work to do. I am perfectly safe in your care, I'm certain." While David was trying to absorb that bombshell, she continued with aplomb. "Please take them off."

The guard cast him a disgruntled glance. "Suppose it's your call, Counselor."

"Thank you."

David rubbed his freed wrists, managing to withhold the outburst until the man was out of the room.

Then he turned on her. "*Counselor?* Are you out of your mind?"

"Maybe," she admitted.

"Don't you have a job to get back to?"

A flash of unease, quickly masked. "I have some time coming."

"Don't I have any say-so?" Probably not. The presumption of innocence, the notion that everyone had basic rights, were only ideas and not reality in his experience.

"Of course you do. In truth, I don't even know if your attorney would allow me to help, but they don't have to know that yet."

He stared at her, questions fighting to get past his lips. "I don't want you here."

She closed her eyes briefly, then tossed her hair and stared right back. "You need me, David—or someone, at least. Surely you don't want to go back to prison."

"Doesn't matter what I want. I'm going. If you'd ask around, you'd know that."

"I have asked. That's why I'm here. I don't think much of the prosecution's case thus far."

He couldn't afford hope. Ruthlessly he strangled it. "The sheriff would have found something on me sooner or later." He shrugged. "Just happened to be sooner."

There was nothing of the insecure, rebellious teen in the look she leveled at him. "This isn't you. What's going on?"

He couldn't let her keep digging. "You don't know me at all. Now tell me about my mother's house."

Her eyes narrowed, but she let the change of subject stand. "It's nearly paid off, only three years left. I can stretch out the schedule, make the monthly payments less. Or I could forgive the debt altogether."

He stiffened. "We don't need charity."

Her raised eyebrows expressed her doubts.

Not that they weren't justified. The alternative was generating more interest charges by extending the term. He didn't like it, but he should be grateful for anything. "I'll manage. Once I know where I'll be sent and what kind of job I'll have, I'll let you know."

Her head cocked. "You're giving up? Just like that?" She frowned. "You can fight this, David. Why aren't you trying?"

He should never have agreed to see her. "You don't

know this place. No one's forgotten Compton. They never will."

"But you didn't start the fight with Patton."

His heart stuttered. "You don't know that."

"I do now." A sly smile quickly vanished. "What aren't you telling me?"

Get out. Go away. "Nothing. I'm done here." He turned. "Guard—" he called out.

She moved fast, grabbing his arm. "I saw the angel."

He jerked from her grasp. He had to get away from her. Now.

"It's beautiful. Thank you," she said softly.

"I didn't do it for you." He'd say anything to get her to back off.

She slipped around in front of him. "I'm trying to help you. To make it up to you, what happened."

"You can't."

"I can try."

His head whipped around. Would she never give up? "Meeting you ruined my life, Callie. Deal with it. I have."

Her eyes went wide in shock. She fell back a step.

David banged on the door until the guard arrived. He got as close to the opening as possible, holding out his wrists. *Hurry up, damn it.*

"I'm coming back. You can leave, but we have to talk."

"Don't bother. I won't show."

"Wait! We haven't talked about your injuries."

"Leave me the hell alone, Callie. You've done enough," he retorted for good measure, then squeezed through the space between the guard and the door frame, wishing he could forget her standing there, slim and beyond beautiful.

Not for him. Never for him. No matter how her scent followed him. How her face haunted him.

What aren't you telling me?

Go away, Callie. It's too dangerous. You have to leave.

CALLIE SAGGED on the bench outside the jail complex. She didn't know what to do. She always knew what to do.

Meeting you ruined my life.

She couldn't catch her breath.

Deal with it.

It was true. She knew that, but damn it, she was trying to help him now, trying to make up for the damage. She'd been the one to come on to him, to lie to him.

She'd been very good at lying. A demon at destruction, so unhappy in her life, so lost and miserable that when a naive, good-hearted boy had reached out to her, she'd yanked him into the cesspool with her. He'd been stunned to find out that she was three years younger, not one, but by then she was pregnant, and it was too late. She'd gotten caught up in the fantasy of Mr. and Mrs. David Langley and refused to consider adoption, abortion, anything but that cockeyed dream of a little family.

What a laugh. She'd have made a lousy mother.

And she hated remembering this, any of it.

Nearly hated him for making her.

Ruined my life.

I did, David. But now I'm going to repay you, even

if I have to fight you to do it. It was all she knew to do to repair the damage.

But how, if he wouldn't talk to her?

She sat up straight. By asking her own questions. Maybe the sheriff was satisfied that he knew the truth. Maybe Capwell was too busy; perhaps David was going to give up without a fight.

But she wasn't ready to. What would she tell Jessie Lee if she did? And David's mother—how could she ever face the woman again?

You owe him. She did.

You can fix this. Jessie Lee's blue eyes so certain. *Who will help him if you don't?* Callie understood the little girl's point. She just hadn't counted on having to battle David, too, in the process.

She was due at Albert's office in a few hours to discuss the further disposition of Miss Margaret's assets. If he hadn't already demonstrated his distaste for David, she'd have sought his advice. For a moment, she contemplated consulting her boss, but she was certain she knew what he would say.

Why would you get involved when you have your own mess to clean up?

But he was also the one who'd ordered her to take some vacation, to make herself scarce for a while.

Callie glanced at her watch and decided to drop in on Randy Capwell again, see if he was around and test the waters about joining him as co-counsel.

Then she would return to Oak Hollow and start asking some questions of her own. She could think of some places to start: David's mother, for one, perhaps going for a drink at the bar where the fight happened, for another.

David might not want her help, but he needed it.

For the sake of what they had once shared, she would play out this hand a little further.

CHAPTER EIGHT

"ARE YOU CRAZY?" TED Bachman, administrative assistant to the D.A., asked her when she called the next morning to test the waters there. "You don't have enough strikes against you, so you jump right into a lost cause?"

She knew better than to call, but she couldn't help herself. She had to touch base with her old life. Anyway, maybe her boss had changed his mind, so she'd started chatting with Ted about David's case. For all the good it had done.

"I have to do this. He's…an old friend."

"Some friend."

What would he say if he knew David had refused to see her today? "It's not a lost cause."

"If it walks like a duck, sounds like a duck, probability's high that it is a duck," he sneered. "C'mon, Callie, Lady Justice doesn't tilt at windmills."

She didn't feel much like Lady Justice lately. "It's hard to explain."

"Cal, you used to be a prosecutor down to the bone. What's happened to you?"

"Nothing. I'm fine." She was still a prosecutor, a

good one. She could leap into her car, be back to the world she understood the next day.

"Maybe it's for the best, though."

A shiver of foreboding crawled down her spine. "What do you mean?"

"Gerald needs a little more time, Cal. You put him in a real bind with that stunt." His uneasiness frightened her. "If you came back now, you'd have to remain low profile for a while yet."

"Low profile?"

"You know, research, behind-the-scenes investigation. Just for a little while."

Grunt work, he meant. She'd paid her dues already. So her choices were to stay away or warm the bench for some undetermined stretch?

Her once-bright future looked murky. She couldn't settle for that. She should return immediately, stake her claim, defend her turf. She was the best; they'd better not forget it.

But if the D.A. was serious about this trip to Siberia, then what? What was her plan? She had a plan, always.

She could start at the bottom again, of course. She'd survive that. She'd screwed up, and she couldn't expect there to be no repercussions.

Okay, she could eat crow. That was better than nothing, right? At least she'd be at the heart of things. If she stayed in Oak Hollow, she couldn't protect herself from those lower on the ladder who were itching to replace her.

Get real, Callie. Grunt work was the province of

neophytes and washed-up burnout cases, not shining stars. Not Lady Justice, even a tarnished one.

"What's really going on, Ted?"

"Cal…" He hesitated. "There are people who are urging the boss to ditch you. The campaign's heating up."

Ah. Now she understood. She was an embarrassment. A liability to his aspirations. *He said he was behind me one hundred percent!* she wanted to yell at Ted.

And wasn't that just naive of her? Hadn't she learned long ago that a politician's promise was as substantial as a dandelion's wispy crown?

"I get it."

"Cal, I'm sorry…" Ted sounded honestly remorseful, but he wasn't the problem. Well, he was, since his fortunes rose or fell with his boss's. "If you'll just stay out of sight a while longer…"

"Don't sweat it, Ted. You know me, right? Tough as nails, the scourge of the courtroom. I'll come out of this just fine, you'll see." She reversed course, chatted breezily about this intern and that assistant, all the office gossip that suddenly seemed so pointless, managing to get off the phone with her poise intact.

Oh, God. Hand still clutching the phone, she stared out the window. *I've fought so hard. If I'm not Lady Justice, who am I? If I lose that, I lose everything.*

Jessie Lee came around the corner of the house, casting a glance toward where Callie stood.

The D.A. had made a promise he might not keep. She'd made a promise, too, regarding David. Was she no better?

And then there were the thirty days Miss Margaret

had asked of her. *Many people will suffer if you don't accept this.*

Callie wheeled away from the window without acknowledging Jessie Lee's presence. She prowled through the small house, feeling Miss Margaret in every room.

He did stuff for her, too. Miss Margaret would want you to help him.

The welcome mat had been yanked away in Philly, at least for the time being. A fix for her situation there was out of her hands. Meanwhile there were people here in Oak Hollow who did need her, whose futures depended upon her actions. She could serve out her thirty days, working hard and, at the end of it, be closer to fulfilling her duty to Miss Margaret. Her great-aunt had actually given Callie a break with her bequest; Callie wouldn't get rich off the rents and mortgage payments in this out-of-the-way burg, but the income, managed right, could buy her some options. Of course she would still return and fight for her job—

But she would have a cushion while she tackled it.

Then there was David. Doing right by him was something positive, something to sink her teeth into, and she was all about action, not standing around.

She had indeed played the pivotal role in wrecking his carefully laid plans for his life, and she owed him. She couldn't change the past, but she could free him now and make a sizable down payment on her debt to him. Whatever he'd been guilty of in the past, he wasn't guilty this time, she was almost certain. She'd need his help in proving it, though, and he wasn't cooperating.

The question was, why?

She needed some means to compel him to partici-
pate, some way to convince him that all hope wasn't
lost. Until the last case, she'd had one hell of a track
record as a prosecutor, so who would understand better
how to find the weaknesses in the case against him?

A solution hit her just then.

She would post his bail. Once outside of a cell again,
he would savor the freedom, would regain hope, would
open up. He'd see that she was on his side, would understand just how good she was. She knew how to win, and
she'd win for him.

And if she proved something to others back in Philly,
too, well that would be a bonus.

Energized by at last having a direction, Callie left to
set her plan in motion.

"WHAT DID YOU SAY?" David blinked at the guard who'd
come for him.

"You're out on bail. Get your ass in gear. Your
mother's waiting for you."

"My *mother?*" Where would she come up with the
money? How had she gotten to the county seat, for that
matter? She hardly ventured from the house. The only
asset she owned besides her worthless car was her home.
If she'd pledged that…

He barely managed to keep a lid on the agitation
brewing inside as they processed him out with painful
slowness, every second agonizing. He cast about in his
mind for a solution, but he didn't think there was any

way to undo the damage. The bitter knowledge that his mother had jeopardized her only security for him ate at him like acid.

When at last he was released through the final door, he was too worked up to dare say anything. With grim focus, he accepted his mother's hug, then hurried to escort her outside. When she handed him the keys to the car, he stared at the ground until he could wrestle his feelings under control.

"Let's go home, son."

He lost the battle. "Why did you interfere? Why would you use the house as collateral? You know they're going to put me away, and I've been trying to save you—" Barely did he clamp off the torrent that wanted to spill.

Frail as she was, she stood against the hurricane. "Drive me home, David. We'll talk after you've rested."

"After—" He looked away. Counted to ten. Twenty. "Mom, I appreciate that you want to help, but I told you—"

"Do you want me to drive?"

He was reminded of the woman who'd had the strength to raise him, who, until Ned Compton, had been the oak that had sheltered him during his childhood.

He hadn't seen that woman in a very long time. Thought she'd ceased to exist.

He shook his head. Opened her door and settled her inside, then rounded the car. He hadn't had a good night's sleep in days, and he was barely rational. Better to save any discussion for later, just as she'd suggested.

He started the engine, registering just for a second the

miracle of being able to drive away when he'd expected to be caged again for a very long time.

"I'm sorry, Mom. I know you meant well."

She patted his hand but remained silent.

He drove them home. Or what would be home for a little while longer.

THE POUNDING ON THE DOOR startled Callie, though it shouldn't have. A glimpse toward the front porch confirmed what she'd been expecting.

It was David. And he was furious.

She straightened her shoulders and crossed to the entrance. "Hello, David."

He yanked the screen door open and stepped inside, his powerful presence filling the room. "What the hell do you think you're doing?"

Apparently he hadn't managed to get any rest once he'd arrived home. His face was shadowed with fatigue, but his eyes were flashing, his generous mouth thinned with resentment.

"I posted your bail," she answered calmly. "As you no doubt know, or you wouldn't be here."

"I told you to leave me alone."

"Actually, I believe your exact words were *I don't want you here.*"

"Don't get cute." His brows snapped together. "Why are you meddling in my life?"

"You're not doing such a hot job on your own, now, are you?" She didn't wait for a response. "You need me, and I have a proposition."

His eyes narrowed. "Explain that."

"Would you like some sweet tea? It's warm today. Come on to the kitchen."

He didn't budge. "Cut the crap, Callie. Tell me what you're after."

"Are you always so suspicious?" She pressed her lips together, regretting what was an absurd question. Why wouldn't he be? "All right. You made it clear that you don't want charity, and I'm not offering it. This is a simple business proposition." She was prepared to use every ounce of persuasion she'd cultivated performing in front of a jury to sell her ideas.

"Go on." For the moment at least, curiosity appeared to be edging past his fury.

"I'm still going to convince you to let me clear you."

"You can try." His expression was bleak, and it got to her. Life had taken a shining boy filled with ambition and dreams and had ground him down to a man who believed in nothing.

"David—"

"Get on with it." A warning, every syllable grated out.

She tried to catch his eye, but he wouldn't look up from the floor, his shoulders tensed. Was he always braced against the next blow?

She took the leap. "I need your help."

His head rose swiftly, his eyes alert for sarcasm.

"Miss Margaret has dumped her whole life in my lap."

"Yeah, tough break, being given all that property."

She flushed. "I've never owned anything but a car. Never dealt with home repairs except to call the super."

She turned up her palms. "I need to understand what there is here, what's needed."

"So call a contractor."

"I don't know anyone. Have no idea who to trust."

"Don't ask me—I've only been back a few months. Get Manning to give you some names."

"I don't want names. I want you."

"Me? Why?"

"Because I trust you, David."

Even as his mouth twisted in a smirk, she caught a flash of vulnerability in his eyes. "Then you're not very smart. Ask anyone. Hell, look at your own experience. How many ex-cons ever deserved to be trusted?"

"They weren't you."

"I clean toilets in a bar. That's all I am."

Her heart twisted. "That's not true, and you know it. Anyway, Jessie Lee tells me you do repairs all the time for her grandmother. That you did them for Miss Margaret." But pleas were obviously not making any headway. "I paid your bail, David."

"I didn't ask you to."

"True, but it's done, and your mother will sleep nights now that you're out." Dirty pool, but whatever worked. She pressed the point. "Will you help me in return? We can settle on a fair wage, and you can work off the debt."

"You expect me to work for you." He gave a short bark of mirthless laughter.

They were probably both thinking about the same thing—their reversals in fortune.

"No. I want you to work for *you*. To help me free you."

"That's not gonna happen. Don't be a child. The deck is stacked, and you can't fix it."

"I think I can. I'm good at what I do."

"You know I don't want this." His voice was low and guttural. "I told you to leave me alone."

Your mother begged me to save you, but Callie didn't dare say that. She held on to her resolve. "Too late now."

Witnessing his struggle was like watching a magnificent wild creature fight his cage, and she found herself wavering. She wondered why she hadn't considered that she'd be trapping him in a different manner, which was maybe no less cruel than a prison.

She nearly opened her mouth to tell him to forget it, though she couldn't take back all that she'd done in her belief that she knew best what he needed.

He spoke before she could. "I'll start tomorrow."

But in his tone, she heard the edge of resentment, tinged with resignation. Maybe despair.

He left with a slam of the screen door.

With a heavy heart, she watched him go.

CHAPTER NINE

CALLIE SIPPED at her coffee as she stood in the backyard, watching a couple of birds fussing over the water in Miss Margaret's birdbath. She'd been up since before dawn, unable to settle as she wondered how she and David could possibly work together. What had she been thinking? She didn't know this man, and she'd gotten her life tangled up with his again, simply on the basis of a child's assurance and a long-ago memory.

Okay, that and the mystery of a wooden angel.

Finding out more about the carving was last on her list of items to discuss now, though. She should stay as far away from the personal as possible. David clearly wished the same, and she operated better without emotion herself.

Distance, that was the key. Professionalism.

There was, however, the small matter of his freedom. She missed her Internet connection; with one, she could e-mail Randy Capwell instead of having to wait until office hours to call him. If, that is, he had e-mail access himself. Surely, he did, though. Georgia wasn't the dark side of the moon, however much Oak Hollow felt like it at times.

Though Callie had no evidence to suggest that David would cooperate in his defense, that was no reason for her to give up. She was not a quitter, and by the end of the day she hoped to be on Capwell's team, at least long enough to get the case on track. If she had to manage the defense herself, she would, even if it meant doing it long-distance. David might believe his case was hopeless, but she could not settle for doing less than everything in her power to clear him, if he were indeed innocent.

Not that his attitude gave her any reason to have hope. Everyone deserved a solid defense, though. If David was guilty, then he should go back to prison. But if not...she had to try her best to clear him. He hadn't hesitated to take her side all those years ago, and she wouldn't be able to live with herself if she didn't return the favor.

A flutter of wings drew her out of her preoccupation as the birds launched into the sky. Suddenly she heard a cat scream, and another one growling.

She nearly dropped her cup in her haste, but righted it before it fell off the porch rail. She charged toward some tall bushes at the edge of the garden, and rounded them. "Hey!"

For a second, the two cats scattered, but then the black-and-white one pounced on the beat-up, scarred old yellow tom. The attacker was young and sleek, and determined, it appeared, to ignore her presence.

She wasn't at all sure getting between them was smart, but there was something about the old cat that roused her sense of indignation. He seemed weak but was still trying to defend himself. When he bared his teeth, she could see that one of the long ones was missing.

"Get out!" she yelled at the bully, who paid her no mind. Callie searched the ground and found a branch that she hoped would be sturdy enough. She moved closer and jabbed at the aggressor. "Leave him alone!"

He turned and snarled, but at least he had let go of the old one.

Emboldened, she stabbed again. "Go away. Shoo!"

At last he scampered off, hissing his displeasure.

She expected the other to run, too. He tried, but his left back leg wouldn't cooperate. "Oh." She started toward him.

"Don't."

She jolted as she recognized David's voice behind her. Despite her resolutions, her heart did a slow somersault as she turned.

She still couldn't get over the metamorphosis from lanky boy to tall, muscular man. He had a presence about him that took up residence right beneath her skin, whether she wanted it to or not.

"Why not?"

"You have no idea what's wrong with that animal. He might have rabies. He could attack you if you get too close. Let him be."

"But he's hurt. I can't just—"

"You'd better. Come on. Walk off so he knows he doesn't have to defend himself from you. See if he can make it on his own."

"But—"

He raised an eyebrow. "You plan on taking him back to the city with you?"

How could she? Pets weren't allowed in her building, even if she had time to care for one. And moving an old cat from this beautiful place to the city… "I guess not."

He studied her for a moment. "Nature doesn't have a bleeding heart."

"Neither do I." She hadn't thought so anyway.

David walked around her, peered behind the bush. "There. He's gone."

"But that other cat—"

"The way of the world." He shrugged it off so easily.

She couldn't do the same, making a mental note to leave some food out in case the injured cat returned.

Then she pulled her attention back to the moment. "You're early." She glanced at her wrist. Only seven o'clock.

The rising sun slanted over his face, throwing his rugged, handsome features into relief. "You didn't say a time." His jaw muscles flexed. "Thought I remembered you as an early riser."

And just like that, the past was a living, breathing entity between them. *Thought I remembered you…* He'd been an early bird, too, and he'd sometimes shared breakfast with her at Miss Margaret's before he'd driven her to school during that fall and winter after the summer that had changed both their lives.

Beneath the bill of his cap, his eyes were too shadowed for her to glean any sense of his mood. *Strictly business,* she reminded herself, but perhaps common courtesy would ease the tension between them. "Would you like a cup of coffee?"

He shook his head.

"I haven't eaten yet. Would you—shall I fix you some breakfast, too?"

Another curt shake. "Just give me your list, and I'll get started."

"I—I thought we could visit each house together. I'd like to hear your opinions as we go through them."

The blasted cap prevented her from seeing his expression, but the stiffness of his shoulders told her a lot, none of it encouraging. "Then I'll work on things around here until you're done." He stalked away before she could respond.

Damn you, David. Stop being a hard-ass. She didn't know whether to put him in his place with a reminder of who was working for whom or leave him alone, as he clearly preferred.

She watched him go, recalling the glimpse she'd had of his despair, his certainty that he was doomed, and found enough patience to say nothing. She should eat to fortify herself for what was certain to be a difficult day. Meanwhile, there was no question that much was needed here at Miss Margaret's to repair the place.

Callie went inside. And left him alone.

VISIT EACH HOUSE. Together.

Of course she couldn't possibly just hand him a damn list. Couldn't let him be and trust him—not when she had put herself in charge of his whole life, now, could she?

No, she had to stand there in front of him, with those big brown calf eyes he'd never fully erased from his mind, the curves of a grown woman replacing the young teen's, with the scent of some expensive perfume that could make a man want to howl at the moon.

Didn't she understand how long he'd been locked up without a woman? How he'd tried losing himself with a stranger one time, only to discover that the purely physical release left him more empty than ever?

Then Callie showed up, and she was nothing like before—*nothing*—yet she kept dragging the past out of the box where he'd had it so firmly locked away.

This isn't you. What's going on, David?

She was gutsy, just as she had been at fourteen, but there was strength in her that she hadn't possessed before. That strength was too tempting to lean on—he hadn't relied on another soul in more years than he could count, and he couldn't start now.

You didn't start the fight with Patton. Her certainty had a lure all its own, if only he could believe in it. She was a temporary fixture in his life, though, and he didn't trust her motives. Something was off-kilter with her, though he couldn't put a finger on it. He didn't have faith in what he didn't know—hell, he didn't have faith in anything, period. The stupid, idealistic boy had learned a lot of harsh lessons behind prison walls, and one of the most enduring was that everyone had a breaking point. No one was as strong as they thought.

He'd go back to jail because he had no choice, and he could survive it again, but he had to enter that zone again where he didn't consider the future and didn't remember the past. He just lived moment by moment until enough days and weeks and years had passed that his time was done.

But hope might very well break him.

Callie, with those big eyes and that slender body and that will of steel, wanted him to hope. Had some crazy idea of defending him. Wouldn't be scared off, however hard he tried to shove her away.

He couldn't say if he'd loved her when they were kids. He'd felt sorry for her, but then, lusting after her, acting on it, had robbed them both of the chance to grow into love. They'd hopped on the high-speed train to adulthood when neither was ready for it.

They'd survived the train wreck, but just barely.

He'd teed off on her unfairly the other day, accusing her of ruining his life. His attraction to her, his own decisions had done that.

But here she was in his life again, and she wouldn't get the hell out. Her courage was as magnetic as her beauty, and he could afford to respond to neither.

She was too damn gutsy for her own good, and he couldn't explain to her why he would have to keep shoving her away.

The stakes were too high if he didn't.

CALLIE WASHED her breakfast dishes and couldn't help looking out the window over the sink more times than she should have.

David was on a ladder, reattaching the gutter to one

corner of the house. From a sheer physical standpoint, he was an impressive specimen.

From a personality standpoint…not so much.

She heard a shout, and his head whipped around. When Jessie Lee skipped into view, his face was transformed by his smile, and Callie's hands fell slack as she watched.

He became another person with Jessie Lee, grinning and teasing as the girl danced around the ladder, gesturing wildly as if telling a story that amused both of them.

Callie couldn't have been more shocked. Or more seized by longing. This was the man her David could have grown up to be.

Was she the difference, the reason he was so surly and distant? Was his resentment reserved solely for her?

Not that she could blame him. The chain of events that had led to his prison sentence wasn't yet clear to her, but there seemed no question that her arrival in Oak Hollow that fateful summer had been the first link. If she hadn't gone out of her way to strut herself in front of him—the town's golden boy, an irresistible target for a girl who fancied herself bad to the bone—would he have granted her a second's attention?

She'd never understood exactly why he'd wanted to spend time with her back then, except for the obvious attraction a willing girl presented to a hot-blooded teenage boy. He'd kept his hands off her with amazing restraint, though, until they'd formed a bond made of long walks over these mountains and quiet conversations of a surprising depth. By the time they'd gone all the way, she'd fancied herself in love with him, even knowing that their romance was drawing to a close.

If it had all ended there, how would they have remembered each other? Who would they be now?

Callie watched David with Jessie Lee and couldn't pinpoint exactly what it was about him that drew her so.

Deeply unsettled by him, whatever the reason, she finished the dishes without looking outside again. Then she headed for the phone to call Randy Capwell to make a case for her participation in David's defense.

"I'M PLEASED to meet you, Mrs. Chambers," Callie said to Jessie Lee's grandmother a little while later.

The older woman fingered her apron. "If it's about the rent…"

"It isn't. We're here to inspect the condition of the property. I want to have a full picture of what repairs need to be done."

Mrs. Chambers glanced past Callie to the silent man at her side. Callie might not have noticed the slight shake of his head had Jessie Lee not spilled the beans when they first met. Callie started to speak but glimpsed Jessie Lee's pleading eyes.

Callie frowned but went along. "Mr. Langley has agreed to help me survey the properties, since what I know about construction wouldn't fill a teacup." She smiled to put the older woman at ease. "My guess is that as Miss Margaret's health declined, she might not have expended as much energy maintaining the properties. If you have concerns, please let me know."

"House is fine, just fine."

Even an unpracticed eye could see that the outside needed painting, so Callie persisted. "Are you certain there's nothing?"

Mrs. Chambers's hand tightened on her apron. "I'm positive. No need to spend any money here." Even Jessie Lee and David tensed.

Then it hit her what the problem might be. Hadn't she been a renter often enough herself to know that when landlords had to pay out money, the rent went up? "Might I speak with you in private, Mrs. Chambers?"

The older woman didn't answer immediately. Squaring her shoulders as if to ward off a threat, she stepped aside in the doorway. "Come in. Jessie Lee, you stay outside with David."

Callie felt the protest from the man in question, though not a word was spoken. She shrugged it off. She was the outsider and not to be trusted. If she were to cross that hurdle, she had to do it on her own. "Your home is lovely," she said to soften the awkwardness. It was painfully neat and scrubbed within an inch of its life, the shabby furniture softened by a jelly glass full of flowers on the coffee table.

"Would you like some coffee?"

"No, thank you. I've already exceeded my limit." Callie smiled and sat. "Please, Mrs. Chambers. I'm not here to cause you problems, I promise." Observing the guarded expression, she went on. "First of all, let me tell you that I have no intention of raising the rent." As the woman seemed to relax slightly, Callie heartened. "I'm new at this, Mrs. Chambers. I'm just feeling my way. I've never owned a home, and neither did my mother. I can only imagine what it's like for you to be raising a growing child, and it's not my intention to make your life harder." She paused to smile. "She's a wonderful girl. You must be proud."

That broke the ice as nothing else might have. "She's a good child, that one. A blessing to me."

Callie seized the opening. "As is David, I would imagine. The help he's given you here."

The woman's eyes darted toward the porch, and her mouth tightened. "Girl talks too much."

"She asked me to help him with his recent troubles, Mrs. Chambers, and she believes you'd want me to, as well. Why shouldn't I know about the good he's been doing?"

A shrug. "It's his choice. Don't know what I'd do without him."

"Do others know?"

"He says it's nobody's business."

"But if they did, people might not treat him so badly."

"You can't let on that you know, Miss Hunter. Not unless he changes his mind."

Callie decided to go for broke. "Do you know what happened to David? The boy I knew…" When the older woman's lips pursed, Callie veered from that path. Bringing up her past wasn't likely to help. "Do you think he's guilty of beating up Mr. Patton? Of starting the fight?"

Rheumy eyes sharpened. "I most certainly do not."

"I don't, either," Callie said. "And I intend to help clear him."

"Good for you." A nod of approval. "Boy needs someone to care."

"Will you help me?"

"How would I do that?"

"I'm not sure yet, but he certainly isn't making it easy."

"Why do you want to get involved?" The older woman looked at her curiously.

"Maybe I owe him."

Another nod. "Maybe you do."

Callie chose not to take offense as she had when David's mother had first charged her with that debt. "All right. I won't mention that I know he's been helping you. Will you let us poke around? You've got enough on your plate, raising Jessie, without living in an unsound structure."

"You really won't raise the rent?"

"Would Miss Margaret have?" Callie turned the question around on her.

"Margaret wasn't a softheaded fool, but she was fair. She tried to work with us as much as she could."

"That's what I want to do, Mrs. Chambers. I want to be fair. Will you give me a chance?"

The older woman studied her for a bit, then she smiled. "I do believe I will."

"Good. Let me go get David and we'll begin."

CHAPTER TEN

BY THE TIME he returned home, David thought a jail cell might be preferable to another day spent in Callie's company. Not that she wasn't pleasant to be with; they'd actually worked together surprisingly well, even peacefully at times. Getting along was worse, though—she was so damned beautiful, so tempting. He was aware of her every second. In another life…

But he was mired in this one. They'd covered only about one quarter of the homes on her list, and he'd wanted to shake her. Couldn't she see that having him accompany her was like attending a tea party with a viper draped around her shoulders? None of those people, with the exception of Jessie Lee and her grandmother, wanted him within a mile of themselves or their families. That Callie insisted on acting as though he were simply her construction advisor and not the most reviled man in town was an advertisement for either her blindness or sheer pigheadedness.

He suspected the latter. He couldn't imagine why she was putting herself through this. She had a job and a life in Philadelphia. She hadn't bothered with Miss Margaret since the day she left.

Why, he asked himself for the thousandth time, was she getting so involved? He knew about the thirty-day provision of the will, but she seemed to be getting deeper into this than she needed simply to satisfy Miss Margaret's condition.

She was so different from the girl he'd known, and he couldn't get a bead on her. She was stronger and more confident, yes, but there was something vulnerable, almost wounded, about her. He'd considered digging to find out, but they'd be better off with less between them, not more. She didn't need to climb into this tar pit with him.

He roamed the house that evening, edgy and itching for something he couldn't define. He didn't feel like reading, and television held no appeal. He thought, for a second, of his carving knife and almost went to the shed out back to search for wood.

Callie kept bringing up that angel, the last piece he'd done. He glanced outside and thought there might be enough light left for him to go take a look at it. See what he thought, years later. He hadn't visited the baby's grave since he'd returned.

He told his mother not to wait up, and though she appeared worried, she only nodded. He set out, needing to burn off energy he was surprised to possess after a long day's exertions.

At last he crossed the grass and stood, thumbs hooked in his jeans pockets, staring at a boy's attempt to smooth out the tangle of his feelings. A part of him lay beneath this ground, and sometimes he felt as if he couldn't draw enough breath as he recalled that pale, still form. *My son,* he thought, barely able to wrap his mind around the notion. *Did I love him?* He couldn't say. He'd been so young, so confused. Callie had been inconsolable, and he'd tried to bury his own emotions to reach out to her, but he'd never had the words, never been able to ease her grief.

My son. His dad, the man David remembered as a smiling, laughing, all-powerful presence in his life, had spoken those words proudly. When he'd died, David's mother had wept many a night in her bed. David had tried to be the man of the house, as much as a boy of eight could understand what that meant.

He saw now that he'd been a child who'd grown up very fast. He'd known the love of a father, and he'd thought to provide the same to his own child, even though he'd had no idea if he could be any good at it.

There was still, David discovered, a dark, empty place inside him where the father in him should have set roots.

Was every parent stunted by the loss of a child? Did they all feel amputated? For him, there was also the shameful scrim of relief he'd felt that he could continue being a kid, that he could go to college—if not with the scholarship that had been promised—believing that a different world, a bright future awaited.

But nothing had turned out that way. Callie's mother had snatched her away without giving him the chance to say goodbye. He'd gotten lost inside his confusion and his grades had continued to plummet. He'd even gotten in some fights.

Then his mother had married Ned Compton to give him a father figure, she'd said, but Compton's brand of fatherhood bore no resemblance to that of the man David had adored. On top of everything, Compton moved them into his fancy house and turned David's mother into someone David didn't know anymore.

David had been lost, so lost. He'd found himself visiting a baby's grave, a baby he hadn't really wanted, and many a night he had tried to speak to that little lost soul. *I'm sorry. I would have done right by you, I swear.* Although maybe it was more accurate to say he would have tried.

In an act of contrition, he'd sought to ease his sense of failure by carving this angel to watch over the child he'd been so ill-prepared to protect.

David squatted before the angel now, his fingers itching to touch it, to trace the lines of it like a blind man. To see if the contact could smooth away the burred edges on his heart.

"It's beautiful, David."

Callie's voice startled him to standing. "What are you doing here?" he said more harshly than he should have.

She retreated a step, looked away from him and into the distance, sadness a heavy veil over her features. "I'm sorry. I'll leave you to it."

"No." He shook his head. "I'm sorry. I—" He swallowed hard. "It's your right to be here."

She shifted and stumbled on the uneven ground. He grabbed her to steady her.

At the contact, both of them went preternaturally still.

It was an innocent touch, holding her upper arm, his

palm absorbing the warmth of her skin. Yet the feel of her was like a door opening to a room with a crackling fireplace and the heady scent of welcome.

He'd been cold for a long, long time.

This was the time of night called the gloaming, when shadows were purple and details disappeared, but she was as real to him, as vivid as at high noon.

Safely shielded inside the violet and umber cocoon, he could focus on her wide eyes, the pupils dark and huge, and hope she didn't notice. He felt the stir of a sense of possibility, the slightest tendril of hope.

"Callie…" His voice wasn't even a whisper, but her nostrils flared. Her lips parted a little, and he leaned toward her until her face blurred and it would be so easy to forget, to cast out doubts, to lose himself…

"David…" Her voice soft and husky, her breath sweet on his face. Her hand rose, touched his side.

Brushed a bruise and plummeted him into the present.

He released her and backed away.

"Please don't." But she, too, closed in, her shoulders rounding. "Don't go yet. I won't…" Her voice trailed off, but he knew what she had been going to say. *Won't touch you again.*

He hungered for the contact though, the humanity. For kindness, but anyone extending that would pay a price. However misguided her good intentions, he couldn't let her fall into that trap. He should be looking for a way to send her running.

Right now he was desperate to be alone, and it was almost completely dark. "It's been a long day." He managed to make his tone carefully neutral, didn't meet her gaze. "Come on. I'll walk you back."

After a brief hesitation, she fell into step beside him. They walked side by side, if separate in their thoughts, for nearly a mile, the moon their only light. When a rut in the road loomed, he took her elbow to guide her around it, letting go the second she was past.

Not a word was exchanged between them, but the night hummed with all they weren't saying. He was unequal to the task of sorting out his own emotions, much less those she might have.

"I would have been a terrible mother," she said suddenly.

He heard the wobble in her voice and stirred himself to respond. "You'd have done fine."

A sad chuckle. "Your memory must be impaired. Don't you remember how utterly screwed up I was? What on earth did I think I could bring to a baby?"

Love, he started to say, but everything he'd felt tonight was choking down his chest, squeezing his heart until a response was impossible.

She didn't speak again for a minute or two, then, "What happened after I left, David?"

For an instant, he actually considered unburdening himself, but the instinct shouting *Danger!* was far too loud. He forcibly reminded himself that he did not know this Callie, could not afford to trust her no matter what yearning this night had stirred in him. He noted their position with relief. "Here's your place. I'll see you tomorrow."

"David—" But she didn't finish, and he didn't respond before he turned away.

But he felt her eyes on him every step down the road, as he cursed himself. And fate.

And Ned Compton.

CALLIE WATCHED David go, fighting the impulse to race after him, but she didn't know if she wanted to invite him in or yell at him or simply hold him. Be held by him again.

When last their bodies had come together, it had been the night they'd buried their child. That night, filled with heartache and pain beyond measure, wasn't one she cared to relive. Especially here and now when she'd stood with him once more over the baby's grave, had seen David reaching out toward the angel as if some sort of salvation waited.

He touched me. Willingly. For a second it had almost been like before.

No, nothing like before. They were different, both of them, but at last—*at last*—the gap had been bridged, if only for seconds.

Some part of him wanted her. Maybe needed her. The yielding of his body, the longing that had arced between them…oh, God, how sweet, how fraught with possibilities.

Her body still echoed with need and yearning. She hadn't been a nun while in Philly, but there had been no one special. No one who reached her as David had, deeper than the physical.

If only she hadn't touched him where he was almost

certainly still bruised from the beating, likely reminding him of his present reality. That had to be why he'd
turned away so abruptly.

More and more, she didn't believe he'd started the
altercation with Mickey Patton. So why was he fighting
her at every step when the deepest yearning of his life
had to be freedom?

Such a tangle, their pasts and their presents. *You don't
have enough strikes against you, so you jump right into
a lost cause?* Ted's questions lingered. But if anything
in the world supported her gut sense that he was innocent, that almost-kiss did. For precious moments, they'd
been David and Callie again, the connection between
them alive and more powerful than ever.

She was reminded of their first kiss years before,
how awkward it had been, yet the sweeter for that. She'd
been trying to seduce him for weeks, throwing herself
at him as inexpertly as only a fourteen-year-old virgin
could. She'd done everything possible to give the illu-
sion of experience because she'd seen something in him
that had spoken to her heart's deepest longing.

He's good, truly good, that tiny wisdom inside her
had murmured.

She'd overplayed her hand. At three years older, he'd
been in some ways a typical sex-crazed boy, yet he'd
possessed a wisdom beyond his age.

She'd never met a boy like him, and somehow she'd
understood that his goodness would fill some of the
gaping holes inside her. Her mother was a lost cause,
and her father was nonexistent. Callie had lived in too

many places and belonged to none. In the only way a mixed-up teen could figure out, she'd used sex to get what she needed.

David had been a gentleman, damn him.

She'd put her crude power on full stun. The lowering fact was that the day he'd finally capitulated had been the day she'd cried. Rough, tough, leather-bedecked and fully pierced Callie had come undone at the sight of an abandoned kitten who'd borne more resemblance to Callie than she wanted to admit. She'd picked it up, and David had driven them to the vet, but the kitten was beyond saving, rail-thin and flea-bitten.

That could have been her, abandoned by her own mother, who'd chosen the party life the second she thought Callie was old enough to stay alone. Callie's final act of rebellion had come after her mother's latest lousy boyfriend had followed her to her room and nearly shoved in the door before she could lock it.

Callie understood now that an inner survival instinct had led her to become enough of a problem to merit drawing attention from those who would demand changes. When her mother was faced with a visit from the authorities to investigate, she'd shuffled Callie off to Miss Margaret's.

And Callie had, unlike the kitten, been saved.

Or she'd thought she had been—until she'd fallen too hard and taken David down with her. The grown Callie grieved that David's descent had begun with her and hadn't yet ended.

But the survivor in her didn't give up easily. It was

the one lesson she'd learned about herself—she was many things, but she was not weak.

She looked off in the distance where David had disappeared, and made a vow.

It stops here, David. Your future will be brighter than your past.

SHE'D SEEN Carl's Corner from the outside before, but Callie had never even attempted to go in it all those years ago. To the kids in Oak Hollow, the bar had seemed a forbidden fruit, enticing perhaps but also a little scary with its nose-wrinkling aroma of stale beer and cigarette smoke escaping every time the door opened.

Now as she entered, Callie looked around with more than a little trepidation. She was no teetotaler or prude, but she preferred her bars to have lots of mahogany and brass, subdued music and sophisticated lighting. This place was the polar opposite—scarred knotty pine walls gone dark with age, neon beer signs on the wall, yellowed light fixtures turning complexions sallow. She was long past the age to be titillated by the rough-and-tumble; she saw plenty of that in her job.

There was a hitch in the hum of conversation when she walked through the doorway. For nearly the space of a breath, she could hear an old Johnny Cash song as if she was standing right by the jukebox.

Her heart slid up into her throat and started choking her.

Or maybe that was the haze of cigarette smoke.

The bartender was staring at her. So were many other sets of eyes.

She knew, deep in her bones, that she'd made a mistake coming here. Why did she forget the way news traveled in a small town? There was no anonymity in Oak Hollow. People probably already knew, God help her, that she'd posted David's bail.

At least he wouldn't be present tonight, not after losing his job.

In or out? That was the simple choice, stay or go.

She decided to stay, and took the first step inside. Sometimes brazening out the situation was the only possible course. She kept her head high and strode straight to the bar. The bartender, a big man, likely an athlete run to fat, gave one curt nod as if admitting her to the kingdom.

Though maybe only on a provisional basis.

Still, she took it. Slid up on a lone cracked vinyl stool at one end of the bar when she would prefer to hide in a booth.

The bartender took his time, sauntering over eventually. "What'll you have?"

Her favorite pinot grigio was probably out of the question. Likewise a mojito or anything of its ilk. "A beer," she answered. "Whatever's on tap." The choice didn't really matter; she was interested in keeping her head, not relaxing.

She surveyed the room through its reflection over the bar. A sparse crowd, but two guys at the pool table in the corner had their heads together, and the glances cast her way weren't reassuring. She wove her fingers together in her lap, clenching them tightly.

The bartender returned with a mug and a coaster. "Three bucks," he said. Then his eyes flicked to the space over her left shoulder.

Callie followed the movement, swiveling on her stool.

A rawboned blond man, younger than herself, touched the brim of his gimme cap. "Evenin', miss. Name's Rudy Ballard. Could I interest you in a dance?"

A bug on a pin could have felt no more trapped as curious glances came her way. "Uh, I don't…" His manner seemed mild, but all her nerve endings were on edge. She grasped at a compromise, pointing to the empty stool next to her. "I just got my beer. Would you care to join me?"

His eyes darted at the change of plans. Behind him, she could see his two pool buddies leering.

The faint blush on his cheeks decided her. "Please." She gestured again. "I'm Callie Hunter."

"I know." Uneasily he took a seat.

Her eyebrows rose at that. "Is that right?"

An awkward shrug made her wonder if he was even out of his teens. "Well, I mean, that is, word travels. Not much going on in Oak Hollow." A toothy smile revealed a dimple in one cheek. "Plus you were at my daddy's house today."

Oh, dear. More and more tangles. "Ballard." She thought for a minute, then recalled the frame house with the half-finished garage under construction. "Oh, yes. I think he said his son was helping him with the new addition. Is that you?"

"Sure is. My daddy has a way with cars, and folks

are always asking him to take a look at theirs. He used to work on Miss Margaret's vehicle, and she encouraged him to set up a real garage there at the house. Went in with him on it." A quick grin. "Said she'd be angling for a better deal on repairs when it was done. Shoot, Miss Margaret knew like ever'body else that there's no better deal to be had, but she liked to tease my daddy 'cause he's so serious."

Callie recalled the man now, tall and sober and silent. His wife, a sweet little bird of a woman, had fluttered about and kept the conversation going while her husband loomed in the background.

"Closest garage after Daddy's is way up to Blue Ridge. Folks need him here, and winter's hard, working outside, lying on the cold ground under a vehicle." Rudy perused her features as others had. She should be used to it by now. "You gonna let me and Daddy finish building? He can't make payments until we get done and he can take more business, but he's good for it, I swear to you."

The responsibility was breathtaking. Miss Margaret's tendrils were wound more deeply into this community than Callie would have ever imagined. "I told your folks I wasn't out to change anything. Did they not believe me?"

Another stain of color. "I don't know. I guess so, I mean—they didn't ask me to talk to you or nothin', but I just, well…" His eyes shifted back toward the pool table. "Folks are worried, seeing you with David Langley and knowing you're from the city and all… nobody is sure what you might do."

He had what trial lawyers called a glass face, his

emotions clear as day. Callie was sure she could get some information from him, but she wouldn't try now, not when the bartender kept wiping the same yard of counter and the fellow two stools down was leaning enough that he could fall with one little push.

"I think I'm ready to dance, Rudy." She stood.

Surprise skipped over his features. "Well, ah…sure thing, Miss Hunter."

"Callie." She smiled up at him and was rewarded by another blush. She walked to the open floor space and turned, waiting for him to follow. "You can call me Callie."

He sped up and gripped her waist with one hand, holding out the other to clasp her palm. They shuffled in a slow box step while she waited for him to relax.

Then Callie the interrogator went to work.

"So what is it that worries people about David Langley?" she asked with just the right touch of wide-eyed innocence. This boy, after all, would have been only a child back then.

His brows flew upward. "Well, um, I mean—" He shook his head, then plunged ahead. "Do you not know he's a murderer? I mean, you come from the city and all, but has no one told you that?"

Her gamble was rewarded. Apparently he was unaware of David and Callie's earlier connection—at least, for now. Plus he was too fixated on her cleavage.

"Well, yes, of course I do, but hasn't he served his time and been released?"

"Yeah." A quick frown as he finally looked at her face

instead of her bosom. "But you've got to be aware that he beat the hell out of Mickey Patton, I mean, I hear tell that you put up his bail."

"I only loaned his mother the money," she lied blithely. "Miss Margaret was apparently fond of him, and I think she would have wanted me to do that. After all, isn't everyone innocent until proven guilty?"

"But he—"

She let her eyes go wide. "Were you here that night, is that it? Did you see the fight?"

"No one did—I mean—" His gaze cut to his buddies.

The sheriff's report said that seven witnesses had sworn David attacked Mickey Patton. There was no way; anyone who'd tried a case knew that seven people would have seven different stories. Witnesses in sync were a suspicious sign, especially when the incident occurred in a bar and at least some of them almost certainly had been drinking. "It's okay. I'm on vacation here, and I've got too much else to worry over." Sometimes the less you pressed, the more you found out.

"We all saw it, just not—" A lift of one shoulder. "Not the very beginning."

She surveyed the room. "There's not much place to hide in here. How come you couldn't see?"

"They were in the alley out back."

"Oh, really." She smiled at him and touched the hair at his nape.

His eyes went a little unfocused. "Um, yeah. I mean, Mickey had had some words with him earlier, but nobody threw a punch in here."

"What kind of words?" Shamelessly she took a deep breath and watched his gaze drop again.

"Mickey, well, he, uh, he's not real easy to get along with. Most folks give him a pass, they don't—"

Hmm. "So Mr. Langley doesn't give him a pass?"

Rudy cleared his throat. "It's not—he doesn't say much. He mostly doesn't come in until near closing, but sometimes when Carl needs extra help, he's here earlier and then he has to be out front. That's when stuff happens sometimes."

"Like fights, you mean?"

"No. Matter of fact, I'm surprised nothing boiled over before. Mickey, he can be downright mean. He's said some things no man would stand for, and me and the boys have wondered how Langley didn't just haul off and pop him."

"Why don't they like each other?"

"Well, see, Mickey, he admired Ned Compton something fierce. My daddy says he always wanted to be a big shot, Mickey did, but in high school, there was David, and nobody could hold a match to him. The whole town was plumb goofy over him like he was the Second Coming or something. But Mr. Compton, when he came to town with his plans to build a resort and provide lots of jobs, he was the real deal, Mickey told me. Folks felt like he could make Oak Hollow someplace special. David didn't like him, though—probably just jealous of Mr. Compton stealing his thunder, least that's what Mickey says. And when Mr. Compton took to courting David's mama, well, David couldn't stand it."

"What does that have to do with Mickey Patton?"

"Mickey took to doing things for Mr. Compton, errands and stuff. Probably just to rile David at first, but he got the notion that Mr. Compton was gonna help him move up in the world, and he wanted that real bad. He said he was gonna be a big man like Mr. Compton and show everybody. So when David killed Mr. Compton, well, Mickey would have led the lynch mob if David hadn't confessed to the crime and gone off to jail right quick."

"So now that David's back, Mickey's still holding a grudge? Has David ever made a move toward him?"

"Not that I saw—" Rudy's eyes shifted to the door, and he stiffened.

Callie glanced over to see a beer-bellied, thick-necked man, his posture screaming aggression.

"That's him, that's Mickey," Rudy said, and paled a little.

"I heard he was in the hospital, half-dead. The stories seem to be a little exaggerated."

"I, uh…"

Just then Patton's gaze landed on her, and she resisted the urge to shiver. Pig-mean, those eyes, as he approached, limping but still menacing.

Rudy skirted away a couple of steps but drew her with him, seeming torn between protecting and abandoning her.

"Evenin', Rudy. Who we got here?"

Callie's spine tingled with the impulse to back away, but she'd learned not to be intimidated, either by her colleagues or the criminals she faced on a daily basis, so she met his gaze squarely. "My name is Callie Hunter." She offered a handshake as if the prospect of his skin against hers didn't make her stomach pitch.

He ignored it as his eyes bored into hers. "I hear you're siding with that son of a bitch who tried to kill me. You got any idea, girl, the filth you're climbing into bed with?" Then his lips curved in a nasty smile. "Is that it? The boy got you back in his bed already? I remember you, see, from back then, sugar."

Never let them see you sweat. She knew that lesson cold. She'd been the target of many crude threats, even some death threats, but never had her skin crawled quite this way. She wanted away from him, wanted a very long shower to wash off any trace of him.

Silence was its own weapon, though never had it been more difficult to wield. She waited several beats until both Patton and his audience had become restless and Patton's neck had mottled with red.

Then, in a tone that was pure contempt, she spoke at last. "It's long been my observation that those most interested in the sex lives of others seldom have one of their own." She kept her eyes on him as one would an adder within striking distance. "Rudy, thank you for the dance. It's been lovely," she said in her snottiest imitation of Main Line superiority.

She could hear the mutters as she grabbed her purse and walked out. She was exceedingly grateful that she was parked near the door.

As she slipped into her car and locked all the doors, Mickey Patton loomed in the doorway.

Shivering, Callie drove back to Miss Margaret's and locked every door and window once inside.

CHAPTER ELEVEN

WHEN MORNING ARRIVED after a too-short night's sleep, she wondered if David would show. Wondered if she dared broach any of what she'd learned last night.

They'd planned another day of inspecting properties, but as she watched the sun rise over the garden, she realized that she craved a day off. Time just to hang around here and…breathe. She was exhausted. It occurred to her that since the moment the ill-fated trial had ended, she'd been on edge, caught in a simmering pot of anxiety—for months before really, ever since the case had come her way.

Callie sank into the old wicker love seat on the back porch, set her coffee cup at her feet and drifted down to rest on her side. Her eyelids descended as she listened to birdsong, felt the brush of morning's still-cool breeze wafting off the hillside. She didn't have the strength to get up and return to bed, and on this shady porch, she didn't really need to move. Each breath came more slowly and deeply than the last, until the world around her faded into an asylum of peace.

DAVID FOUND HER asleep when at last he arrived twenty minutes late. He hadn't intended to come at all, but conscience had warred with instinct, and conscience had won.

He'd knocked on the front door with no resulting answer, so he'd walked around back, expecting to find her as before, somewhere near the garden. Not that she had the first idea what to do with it.

He'd almost called out to her, but he was glad now that he hadn't.

He stopped and considered leaving, but he didn't do that, either. He owed her for his bail, and whatever sins could be posted to his account, reneging on his debts would not be one of them. That was only part of the reason he was here.

This was the first time he'd had a chance to take a good look at her without her knowing, and though it could be considered an invasion of her privacy, he was going to do it anyway.

He needed to understand her. He was driven to figure out how the connection between them—God knows he'd felt the punch of it last night—had survived when nearly everything about them was different.

David inched closer to the porch but remained on the ground, his gaze traveling over her with haste, as a starving animal bolted down food without tasting it for fear it would disappear. Once he'd covered her head to toe, he started again, only slower.

She was beautiful to him, but he thought she might just be beautiful, period. Only a minute examination of her features revealed anything familiar.

But last night she'd seemed, for the first time, like the real Callie, the soft girl pretending to be tough, the one who was strung so tight with misery, who felt that there was nowhere on earth she belonged.

That girl, so tiny and thin, had grown into a stunning woman who gave every appearance of command over her life and her circumstances, instead of being whipped by the winds of fate as had once been the case. The Callie who'd snarled and tried to bite every helping hand but his, he'd thought her completely vanished.

Until the grown Callie's composure had cracked over a baby's grave.

It was so hard to keep the Callies straight, to remind himself that just as he was forever changed, so might she be. That the girl who'd blossomed under simple attention, who'd found her laughter again—buried as it had been under black leather and ugly boots—that girl was lost to him, and their bond forever slashed.

This Callie, the grown one, the harder one, he did not know and he could not predict. The call of her, the lure she presented, must be blocked out, could not be trusted.

No one could be trusted, not now. Not with the secret he would carry to his grave.

David realized then that he'd begun to relax his guard, that he had to back away, get out. Now.

But just then, the breeze shifted, and the scent that came to him blasted away all his good intentions.

"WHY DOES YOUR HAIR smell like cigarette smoke?"

Callie struggled from her fog and saw David's eyebrows drawn together, fierce and furious. "Excuse me?"

"Answer me. Where did you go when I left you last night?"

"And why would that be any of your business?"

His eyes narrowed. He cursed, long and low. "Damn it, Callie. There's only one place in Oak Hollow with that combination of beer and smoke. What the hell were you doing at Carl's?" He shot to his feet, prowled the back porch, every step echoing anger.

Then he whirled. "Do you not have a lick of sense? Don't tell me you went there alone." He cast a look upward as if pleading with the heavens. Just as quickly, his attention snapped back to her. "Of course you did. I told you to butt out, didn't I?" When she remained silent, he repeated himself. "Answer me—didn't I tell you to stay out of this?"

"I am trying to help, you rock-headed fool. You're going to jail if I don't. Your attorney means well, but he's way overloaded."

"You said you wanted my advice."

"On construction, not on your legal defense. That's my arena."

He bent closer, the skin around his mouth strained white. "But you're not my attorney, now are you?" When she didn't respond, his eyes widened. "What have you done, Callie?" His voice was low with horror. "No." He shook his head violently. "No, goddammit. There has to be one thing about my life that I control. Tell me you haven't taken action to become my lawyer."

She swallowed hard. Dodged. "I can't legally represent you, not alone."

"Oh, sweet mother of—" He paced again. Wheeled on her. "What were you doing at the bar, asking questions?" He frowned. "Who was there? Was Patton?"

She glanced away. "It was fine."

He grabbed her elbow, swiveled her to face him. "He was, wasn't he? Damn it, Callie, that's not only stupid, it's dangerous. *He's* dangerous. You stay away from him."

"I deal with murderers and rapists and drug dealers all the time. There is nothing in Oak Hollow that can come close to the scum I've seen."

"And you're in the middle of them, all alone? Bullshit, Callie. Don't talk down to me. I've lived with criminals like that for fifteen years. I've been surrounded by them, been in the middle of their depravity, the wars waged only because someone's skin is white and someone else's is black." His eyes were dark then, haunted and hollow.

More than ever, she was forced to face what it would have been like for a tender boy to be thrown into the midst of that sewer. She knew what it was to want to scrub your skin raw to remove the taint. To gulp huge breaths of outside air.

But he'd had no visitor's pass to let him escape. Her heart hurt for that boy. Whatever his crime, he could not have been prepared for the cesspool that had closed over his head that first day.

Watching her closely, his eyes went to slits. "Don't you feel sorry for me," he growled. "I won't have your pity."

"I'm not." But she had. She did. She was all too familiar with the misery, the sheer animal rage that simmered inside those walls. She pictured David in there, and the horror of it was fresh and new. How could that big, open heart of his have survived the massacre of the soul that was prison?

It couldn't, of course. She felt sick to her stomach at the waste of a bright mind and a sweet, pure soul.

And watching him, she could see the taint of those years, the shame he felt at her new awareness of him.

He looked stricken. Vulnerable as he had been when he'd discovered her coming out of that monk's cell bedroom in his mother's home. If she'd stripped him naked and paraded him through the streets, it wouldn't have been more degrading, she realized. "David—" She reached for him, wanting to comfort, longing to soothe him, to tell him she understood.

He yanked from her grasp with an expression of such loathing she felt dirty. He stepped off the porch and started walking away.

She didn't know what to say. How to fix this.

But she couldn't let him leave, not like this. "David—" She scrambled after him, trying to catch up with his long strides. "David, I don't—" Finally she had to run to close the gap. She grabbed him again.

He turned on her. "Stay away from me." His voice was low and dark and menacing, and he loomed over her. "Do you hear me?"

"I'm not afraid of you." But her voice wavered before she could firm it. She had to right this grievous wrong. She cleared her throat, sought out every last bit of composure she could salvage. "I don't pity you, I swear it. I—I don't understand what happened back then, but the boy I knew—"

"Is dead. Never forget that."

She didn't respond to that. He was talking to her, that was all she'd focus on. "I can't do anything about what you've been through, but I can help you now. Convince me that you started that fight with Mickey Patton, that you intentionally beat him up. Do it, David, and I'll let you be." Her chin jutted. "I have a mess of my own to clean up back in Philly and all these loose ends here. I have plenty to do, and I'm no bleeding heart. I'm a prosecutor. I put scumbags away, and I'm good at it. If you're one of those, I'll gladly shut the cell door and turn the key, but my instinct says there's more going on here. You could explain everything to me, and I wouldn't have to go to places like Carl's to save your stubborn hide."

He stared off into the distance, a muscle in his jaw flexing. Then he looked down at her. "What kind of mess?"

"What?"

"In Philly."

"None of—"

One brow arched. "My business?"

She opened her mouth. Shut it again.

Just then, they both heard Jessie Lee singing, the sound growing louder as she approached the back of the house.

"You asked for my help with these properties," he

said. "That's all the business we have together. You don't pry into my life, and I won't pry into yours. You want to go back to Philly, then stop screwing around playing lawyer and let's get this over with."

"But—"

"Hey! You're both here," called out a cheery young voice.

"You've already butted into my life too much. I'll pay off my bail, then we're done. Take it or leave it," he said, too low for Jessie Lee to hear.

"Callie? David? Y'all okay?"

She was the first to look away, summoning up a cheer she didn't feel. "We're just fine. How are you this bright morning?"

Giving David her back but not her promise, Callie walked over to join the girl.

If his looks had been daggers, she would have been bleeding half to death.

CHAPTER TWELVE

THE OLD MAN MET THEM at the door. "What's he doing here?"

"Mr. Langley is with me, Mr. Sims. We're inspecting the properties Miss Margaret left me."

"Uh-uh. Not having a murderer in my house. Man nearly beat my nephew bloody when he tried to help Mickey."

Callie didn't have to look back to feel David stiffen. She wondered which one of Mickey Patton's drinking buddies this man was related to. "Mr. Sims..." she began.

"You get the hell off my property," the old man interrupted. "You ought to still be locked up. Ned Compton was going to save Oak Hollow. Town's suffered ever since."

"That's enough, Mr. Sims." Callie glanced back and saw David's jaw harden, his green eyes flare. For a second, she considered leaving, but then she realized that this man might have information that could impact David's case. She needed anything she could get, but antagonizing him would gain nothing, so she made a choice. "Would you please excuse us?" she said to David. "I'll catch up with you at the next place, all right?"

David went utterly still, and one glimpse from him made her feel queasy at the cost to him. His shoulders were ramrod straight as he turned on his heel and left without a word.

"Miss Margaret would be ashamed of you, keeping company with a criminal, young lady."

Callie bit her lip until it hurt. "May I come inside?" she asked instead. "I'm trying to take good care of Miss Margaret's estate, and I'd appreciate a few minutes of your time to discuss your situation."

"I missed only one payment."

"I'm not here to cause problems, Mr. Sims. I simply want to talk a little and see what we can work out."

"Invite her in, for goodness' sakes, Hiram," said a female voice from behind him. "I'm Luella Sims. You'd be Miss Margaret's niece. Please come in. Would you care for some sweet tea on this hot morning?" The woman was tall and big boned, her hair a silver helmet.

"Thank you. I'd appreciate that."

"I'll be right back. You just have a seat."

Her husband grudgingly escorted Callie to a sofa dotted with floral chintz pillows, then took his own seat in a rump-sprung recliner. Arrayed on top of the television were several photos of various adults and children. "Your family?" she asked.

He shrugged a shoulder and only grunted.

Mrs. Sims bustled back in with a sweating glass, placing it on a crocheted doily atop the coffee table in front of Callie. "Yes, our three girls and their babies. Seven grandchildren in all." She beamed.

This could be her source, Callie realized, so she sought for the correct response, though her store of small talk was sorely lacking. "They're very cute."

"Bright as pennies, every one of them. Tim here—" She touched one photo of a boy maybe around Jessie Lee's age. "He's already decided to be a lawyer."

"Boy could argue the day of the week and convince you," grumbled his grandfather, but there was pride in his tone.

Callie wondered if pointing out that she was an attorney would help or hinder her aim. "I'm a prosecutor back in Philadelphia. You might advise him to enter debate competitions. That looks good on law school applications."

"Why, isn't that a grand idea and good of you to mention?" said Mrs. Sims. "We'll just do that, won't we, Hiram?"

He only jerked his head, but Callie thought maybe she saw a little softening.

She was quickly disabused of that notion. "What's a prosecutor doing, going around with a criminal?"

Callie once again suppressed a heated response. "I'm sorry about your nephew, but it's not my case to try, and the law says a man is innocent until proven guilty. Miss Margaret had Mr. Langley perform various repairs, and I asked him to use his knowledge to help me figure out what to do with the properties she entrusted to me."

The old man bristled, but his wife interceded. "Would you like a tour of the place?" She stood. "Weren't you headed for the post office, Hiram?"

Practically before Callie could blink, Hiram Sims had been whisked out the door and she'd been presented with a plate of lemon cookies, along with her glass of tea.

"David's mama's a good woman. Folks are upset because they believed in David, even set up a fund to help him with college expenses. Then he went off the track after—" She pursed her lips. "Well, it's a shame, is all, but he's kept his head down since he came back. He hasn't made any trouble, just stayed to himself, up to now." She leaned closer. "Hiram's sister's son spends too much time with Mickey Patton. That man was a bully as a child, and he hasn't improved with age."

Mrs. Sims paused for breath, but it didn't last long. Callie listened and absorbed every word.

ONCE SHE REJOINED DAVID, he had little to say to her the rest of the uncomfortable afternoon, restricting his comments to construction issues and even then parsing each word as if he had a limited supply.

But at last, they were done with the inspections. "I'll work up an estimate of the cost for the work I'm able to do. Some of it will require skilled tradesmen, and I can't help you with suggestions for that. I've been away too long to know who to recommend." He snapped shut his notebook and started for his mom's car, then turned back. "I don't have a truck to transport materials, either. Deliveries to Oak Hollow from the nearest lumberyard aren't cheap, I'll warn you."

Callie glanced at the vehicle he was driving,

clearly not his own choice, and squirmed for him. How many blows to his pride could a man take and still remain standing? Yet despite the constant antagonism and his generally ignominious circumstances, David did not falter. There was steel in his spine and power shimmered around him. She'd admired the boy he'd been, but the man was even more impressive.

"David…"

He halted but kept his back to her.

I won't have your pity. She knew he didn't want her help, but she was desperate to make up to him for the damage she'd caused.

It wasn't pity, not really. Guilt yes, buckets of it.

But that he didn't want to discuss it anymore was evident, so a thank-you was what she allowed herself.

One curt nod, and he left.

Callie watched until he was out of sight. Then, dispirited, at last she climbed into her own vehicle.

And barely resisted the urge to keep on driving until she left Oak Hollow and all its memories behind.

OH, HOW SHE HATED the nights when sleep eluded her. She'd had too many of them, stressing over a case, giving her closing arguments again and again until the bed had seemed a prison and she'd kicked her way to freedom, only to find her apartment walls suffocating. Sometimes she'd pace and talk herself down; other times she'd exercise herself into exhaustion. Often she'd have preferred to go for a run, but she didn't live in a neighborhood that lent itself to midnight rambles. She'd chosen it for efficiency, as it was close to work and had plenty of places to eat out.

Because work was where she actually lived.

Callie tossed again, punched the pillow. Finally sat up before she could scream. She'd slept well enough here up to now, but tonight…

She kept seeing David's face, the despair in it. The determination overlaying that. The stubborn sense of honor others seemed to miss. Not Jessie Lee, though, or her grandmother. And not Miss Margaret.

Callie rose abruptly and began to pace. She glanced out the front window and saw only a smattering of lights from porches and utility poles in yards. Oak Hollow was not a big city; more than likely she was the only soul awake at this hour.

She could walk outside right now, clad as she was in a nightgown. The notion had her lips curving. She thought Miss Margaret, the quiet rebel, might get a kick out of it.

So out onto the front porch she went, straight to the edge of the steps. She stood there, head swiveling from side to side, eyes alert, ears perked and waiting for what she did not know. She moved along the wraparound porch, headed for the wicker love seat.

She heard a noise off to the left. At first she thought it might be the missing tomcat, but this sounded completely different, sort of slithery and menacing. She skittered to the side, her heart thumping. All of a sudden she was afraid to put one bare foot in front of the other, and the expanse between her and the front door seemed a football field long.

The love seat by then was only one leap away. In a split second she'd landed on it, had her feet off the boards and her legs tucked beneath her.

She shivered and wished for a blanket. Mountain nights were cool, but she was not, no sir, stepping one foot from where she sat. God knows what might be out there—or what had possessed her to leave the safety of the bed.

In that moment, Callie missed squealing tires and yelling neighbors and sirens and boom boxes. Those noises she understood.

Wild things she did not.

Oh, mercy, something was moving in the grass, something that slithered while something else scratched. She uttered a small scream. She had to get inside. The back door was locked, though. If she ran really fast, she could surely outrun whatever was out there that might bite or sting or claw or—

Callie took off running pell-mell around the porch, desperate for the safety—

"Oof—" She hit a solid wall and screamed again.

"Callie." A gentle shake. "Callie, you're okay. Hush now. You'll have the neighbors out with their guns."

Warmth registered. A voice, human.

Male.

"David?" She couldn't help it, she started shaking, whether from fear or relief she couldn't say. She grabbed on, dug her fingers in his jacket, slid her hands around his waist and burrowed.

"Hey, there. What happened? What did you see?"

She stood on her tiptoes and stretched, wanting her bare feet off the boards, away from whatever the noises had been. Scrabbled her fingers as if to launch herself upward.

Then he lifted her. "Are you hurt?" He tried the back door, then walked with her around to the front and shouldered inside. "Let me look." He flicked on the closest lamp, and Callie was blinded by the faint light.

Quickly he rounded the sofa, then laid her on it. "Talk to me, Callie."

She became aware that he was fully dressed and she was barely covered. She scrambled to sit up in the corner of the sofa and pulled a throw pillow in front of her. "I'm okay. It was just…" She shrugged. In the glow of the lamp, her fright faded. "I have no idea what it was." She gave him a rueful grin. "I…there are so many sounds here, yet it's unnervingly quiet, too."

He nodded and smiled back. "When I first got back…" Dark shadows floated across his eyes. "Never mind." He looked away.

She was so tired of him eluding her, of never making a connection. "Prison and cities have some things in common—noisy and always simmering." Maybe tackling his past broadside would help.

His look was full of speculation. "Never thought about it that way." A pause. "I've never been in a city, so I couldn't say."

She was struck dumb, newly aware that in his whole life, he'd lived only in two places—Oak Hollow and the prison at Jackson—but pity was out of the question. "I saw something move in the grass, and I could swear I heard a slither." Just the memory made her shudder.

"It was only a skunk, though I spotted a possum, too."

"That's all?" She felt vaguely insulted. "I got scared half to death by two little animals?"

A quick grin. "A skunk's no laughing matter if he sprays you."

"What a city girl I am." She shook her head. "Embarrassing." Then she frowned. "What are you doing here?"

"Out running. Heard you yell."

Callie flushed. For the first time she realized that he'd been unusually warm and registered the triangle of sweat on his shirt. Then that broad chest became all she could see.

"Why are you running at night?" She yanked her eyes away from all that muscle.

"Couldn't sleep."

"Really? Me, neither."

Silence landed between them with a thud, but it had teeth and toenails, clawing its way beneath her skin and reminding her of too much.

She sought a diversion. "I have trouble sleeping," she admitted. "I used to run on a treadmill. Safer place in a city at night."

"Less likely to break your neck, that's for sure." But his tone held a hint of challenge.

She cocked her head. Wondered where the daredevil girl had disappeared to. "Can I come with you?"

He was momentarily nonplussed. "Now?"

"They say vigorous activity before sleep is a lousy

way to get your rest." Then she wanted to slap a hand over her ungoverned mouth when she realized how *vigorous activity* could be construed.

A quirk of his lips, a light in his eyes. "I always wondered who 'they' were."

The lighter tone compelled her to string out the teasing a little longer. "On the other hand, 'they' aren't here."

The moment sang with awareness…of the dim light, of the darkness beyond it…of the fragile truce. Callie was afraid to breathe for fear of disturbing it.

He seemed to share her reluctance.

"Or we could play gin rummy."

His head jerked up. "Play…cards?"

She'd surprised him. "A nice gentle game of gin might just send us both straight into the arms of Morpheus."

"Hypnos," he said. At her start, he explained. "The father of Morpheus and the god of sleep. Morpheus was the god of dreams."

She was quickly reminded that he'd been not only the best athlete but the smartest kid in his school. Grief for that boy flickered, but she would not let it ruin this odd peace between them.

"No gin. You got anything but stilettos to put on your feet?"

"You must not have been paying attention to the Oak Hollow grapevine. Jessie Lee nearly died from excitement when the FedEx truck made its way up the mountain to deliver my clothes." Then she hissed at the memory of the afternoon and how they'd parted. And what the grapevine had done to him.

But the wispy truce held. This out-of-time moment continued.

"Any running shoes in it?" he asked.

Since that was the extent of her sensible shoes, she'd made her running shoes and her favorite jeans the top of her list, and her assistant Anna had come through for her. "Yes."

He rose. "Ten minutes enough?"

She rolled her eyes. "I'll see you in five." She lifted her chin and pretended she was wearing a power suit and not a thin scrap of fabric, forcing herself to walk past him and not run.

But the second she was in the hallway, she took off.

Before this David, so poignantly like the one she remembered, could vanish on her.

CHAPTER THIRTEEN

HE'D NEVER RUN with a girl, David realized. *Woman,* he corrected himself. Callie was definitely no girl.

He was forced to adjust his long stride or leave her behind, but not because she was in poor physical condition. Quite the reverse, her breathing was steady, and she held her head high as she focused on the road ahead.

"There's more light than I would have expected," she said. Her lips quirked. "Guess I'm too accustomed to streetlamps. You seldom see stars in the city, and this moon is really bright."

"I wouldn't have brought you out here if it hadn't been a full moon."

She looked over at him with a curious expression. "No, you wouldn't have, would you? I remember that about you. Always the protector."

The warmth of her gaze was a caress. He indulged himself in it for a second.

Move on. There's no future here. "These old roads are too uneven," he continued. "Pockmarked by winter, and the only maintenance is what the locals do for themselves. This county's too sparsely populated for a decent tax base."

"I forget sometimes." At his wrinkled forehead, she explained. "That you always paid attention to so much outside yourself."

He shrugged off the compliment, but she persisted. "You were forever seeking out information about all kinds of topics, and you were interested in so much more of the world than many teenagers. You're still one of the most intelligent people I've ever met."

He didn't know how to respond, so he said nothing.

"Did you—" Abruptly she stopped, and he braced himself for a return to the conversations about his case.

But she surprised him. "Did you have things to read in there, David? Were you able to take your mind away?" She slowed her steps. Halted. He had no choice but to stop, too. "Can we talk about this, or is it too painful?"

He looked down at her earnest expression, her skin ivory in the moon's glow, those milk-chocolate eyes round and soft. He reached out slowly and brushed one stray curl back from her forehead.

She didn't flinch from his touch but closed her eyes instead.

Those lips tempted him so. One kiss, just one…

He stepped back. *No future.* He had everything to lose by starting something that would have to end. He began to run again.

Soon she joined him. They ran for a while in total silence, only the sound of their mingled breaths disturbing the night.

When he'd locked his yearnings far enough away, he sought to make amends for his brusqueness. "The prison library wasn't too bad." He felt her attention like a physical caress. "The librarian took an interest in me, and after a few years, he requested that I be allowed to become his assistant." He thought of Earl Rasmussen with a mixture of gratitude and fondness. "He was a retired classics professor, convinced he could save the prison population single-handed if he could just get everyone to read the works that had endured the centuries." At that, David found himself smiling.

"Did he?"

"No, but he was a sneaky old man. He brought in comic book versions for the hard cases and hooked them that way first. He actually got a reading group started, and some of the guys who'd dropped out of school in junior high did make the transition from superheroes to mythology."

"He sounds wonderful."

"He was. He gave me a window on the world. We spent a lot of hours talking while cataloguing or repairing books. He could argue any side of any issue." *He saved my life.*

"Is he still there?"

Fond memories plummeted, smashed on the rocks of reality. "He died stepping between two inmates to stop a fight."

"I'm so sorry."

"Yeah." The old debris began rising. *Lock it down.* The sweet, clear night tarnished under the smear of his filthy past. "Let's turn around. It's late." He did so without waiting for her, and he no longer shortened his stride as much, though he stayed close enough to be sure she was all right.

The high tide of destruction wouldn't be held off forever, though. He could hardly wait to get her back to her place.

When they arrived, he stood like a sentinel, expecting her—needing her—to go inside right away.

"David, I'm sorry. I didn't mean to make things worse."

"It's not you," he managed. *Can't you see, Callie? Everything I touch turns foul.*

She stepped closer. He stepped back.

She grabbed his forearm before he got too far. "What you've been through—no one comes out without marks. I know that world as well as someone not locked inside it can." Her grip tightened, and as much as he longed for it and knew he shouldn't, God help him, he didn't shake her off. "You can talk to me about it. I won't be shocked. The universe I've operated in...there's not much that can rattle me anymore." She slid her hand down and grasped his. "We don't know what's inside us, what we can do if we're pushed, not until..." Her eyes became distant and haunted. "Not until we're faced with one moment, one instant..."

He stopped breathing. Could she know? Could she really understand if he told her, if he gave up his most buried secret? For a moment David felt a nearly irresistible temptation to take that chance, to at last let someone see.

But in that same second he thought of the person who would be destroyed by the truth, and he knew that, yet again, he would swallow the words that had choked him for fifteen endless years. "I can't, Callie." He heard the hoarse voice that hardly sounded like his own.

He clasped her hand for one bittersweet beat, then let her go. "Thank you, though." He could give her that much. Owed her that. Especially when, by withholding his own confidence, he was denying her the chance to share her burdens. *You can talk to me if you need to,* he almost said, but couldn't afford to.

They had no future. They could come no closer.

"I hope you can sleep now." He turned away like the loser he felt himself to be.

She said nothing, which he deserved.

He ran home, every step dogged by his yearning to turn back.

SHE DID SLEEP WELL. Even though heartache had accompanied her to bed, her muscles were warm and lax and she'd barely managed to change out of her clothes before her eyelids had closed.

Now, as she stretched in bed and listened to birdsong, she let her mind range over the night before.

David was hiding something, the conviction grew within her. He was fighting himself…but why? She went over all that they'd said during the run, picking at it for hidden treasures, tiny gems of truth that would provide new pieces to the puzzle that was David.

Maybe he'd simply become that private. Even as a teen, there had been depths to him, yes, pockets of maturity beyond his age. But no secrets, she would swear to that. He'd been a young man filled with confidence in his own abilities, a leader both of his football team and his school, liked by everyone. He'd been under great pressure to be Oak Hollow's shining star when he moved out into the world, but he'd borne even that with grace.

She'd watched David minister to lost cats and lonely old ladies. He'd accepted the burden that the town placed on him with no complaints or self-pity. He'd had his ambitions—a lot of them, in fact—but he hadn't fought the ambitions others had for him; instead, he had simply incorporated them into his load and moved on.

So what could have broken him? What had made the amiable teen turn into a self-confessed killer?

Her musings were interrupted by a catfight right outside her window. If that interloper was running off her scarred old tom again…

Callie leaped from the bed and charged outside, grabbing a broom along the way. "You leave him alone, you little creep!"

Sure enough, the sleek, muscled juvenile delinquent was on the attack. She ran after the aggressor. "You get out of here, you hear me?" Barefoot on cool morning grass, she bent and tried to soothe the old tom, who rewarded her with a swipe of his claws and took off like greased lightning.

"Well," she grumbled, settling back on her heels. "You remind me of someone else who doesn't appreciate my help."

"Ouch," said a very familiar voice behind her.

Callie jumped to standing. "David! What are you doing here?"

"Thought I'd fix that kitchen faucet of yours before I got started on the Chambers house. They're not quite ready for me."

His gaze skimmed over her, and abruptly Callie realized that she was outside in a tank top and flannel drawstring pants that hung low on her hips, leaving both her arms and a wide strip of abdomen bare to the chill.

And her nipples were standing up. She crossed her arms over her chest, but that still left other parts of her exposed. "Oh. Ah, well, um…I'll go make coffee. Want some?"

When she finally met his eyes, he was actually smiling.

Just a simple smile, but relaxed and easy for a change, with a little spark thrown into the mix. The very normalcy, along with the absence of anything like it from him since they were teens, gave that smile a punch that socked her right in the solar plexus.

"Yeah, I would." Something more in his heated gaze had her wondering if he could possibly be interested in more than coffee.

Down, girl. So far, he'd been the master of the mixed message. Stay—go. Start—stop. Leave me alone—come here. Kiss me. Don't touch me.

And she was little better, she had to admit.

Oh, stop thinking so much. Just let the moment stand, would it kill you?

Maybe not. She'd always been lousy at living in the moment, but nothing else was working, and she was tired of the constant struggle.

So she smiled right back and was rewarded by an increased wattage in his. They stood there like that until a breeze made her shiver, and she realized that her feet were wet with dew and the hems of her pajama bottoms were rapidly getting that way.

"You better cover up," he said, but his voice was warm and a little husky.

"I guess I should," she responded. But for a second or two longer, she stayed right where she was.

Until the wind picked up and ruffled her hair, sending a chill across the back of her neck and woke her from her sensual trance.

"Coffee."

"Coffee." He nodded.

"Be right back," she said.

"Stay inside where it's warmer," he responded. "I'll get my tools and fix that faucet."

"Okay." She didn't move.

"All right." He didn't, either.

At last he broke into a full-fledged grin and turned her with a gentle push. "Get inside, Callie, before you turn into a Popsicle." He strode off toward the shed.

Maybe then you could come and warm me, she thought.

She hadn't been truly warm in a very long time.

"CAN I DO THAT?"

"What?" David wished Callie would back away. She was dressed now at least, but he'd come in from the shed to hear the sound of the bathtub running, then waited for the coffee to finish dripping while listening to too-intimate splashes from behind the connecting wall. With each silvery slide of water, he could so easily imagine the trail of moisture over the curve of her breasts, the slickness of pale skin that had barely been interrupted by the skimpy tank. Her belly was smooth and toned, her hips a feminine curve that taunted his hands….

"…the faucet. I'd like to try it myself."

David yanked himself back from the fantasies he could ill afford. Vigilance had been everything for fifteen years, and now was no less treacherous. "You want to learn plumbing?"

She was bent over the kitchen sink, her jeans tight and low-slung, her equally formfitting T-shirt riding up to reveal again that sweet strip of skin that had his fingers burning to touch. She glanced over at him, and he didn't tear his gaze away fast enough. Her eyes asked questions while her sweet lips formed words he barely registered. "If I'm going to own property, I should understand how things work. I don't like to rely on others much."

She'd been like that before, stubborn and independent, impatient with being so young. "That's wise." He dragged himself all the way into the present, past lips he hungered to kiss, flesh he yearned to caress.

Hadn't he spent the night lecturing himself about what was possible? He cleared his throat. "This is simple really. The first thing to do is to study what you have, get it fixed in your mind before you take it apart. Then focus on each step and lay out the parts you remove in a line, so you know the order to replace them."

She gnawed at that full lower lip, and he thought he

might lose his mind. He busied his hands with plumbing parts instead of flesh. "I'll put back what I've done and let you try."

"Really?" Her eyes shone with delight. She bent closer as he worked, and he could smell her, no fancy perfume, only soap and woman. She had no makeup on that he could tell, and she needed none to take a big bite out of his control. His fingers lost their coordination, and his wrench slipped, scraping the knuckles of one hand. He cursed beneath his breath.

"Oh! You're bleeding. Here, let me…" She clasped his hand in hers, breathing warm air over him. "I'll get bandages."

He jerked his hand from hers. "It's nothing."

"You need to protect them from further injury."

"I said forget it, Callie."

She looked hurt. Her delight dulled. "I should go." She stepped back.

He muttered another curse. Exhaled. "No." It wasn't her fault her nearness was driving him crazy. "I'm sorry. You're right. It's sensible to protect the scrapes before I get more dirt in them." He had to stop sounding so testy; she was only trying to help. "Thanks."

Subdued, she left the room. He stared outside, wondering how he would get through whatever days he had left before she was out of his life again.

"Here." She proffered a box of ancient bandages. "I guess Miss Margaret didn't use these much. I could go to the store…"

"These will be fine." After a beat, he added, "Thank

you." Then he concentrated on trying to use his non-dominant right hand to apply the first one but he only managed a poorly fitted wrapping.

"Do you want help?" Her voice was hesitant.

He glanced up. Nodded. "If you wouldn't mind." It was torture, sheer torture, his rough hands being caressed by her slender soft ones. Watching the curls that were more evident each day as she shed some of the city veneer and wanting to bury his fingers in them, to lift her face to his and taste her—

His fingers curled involuntarily, and Callie looked up, worried. "Did I hurt you?"

He couldn't speak, only shook his head. He tried to relax, to beat back the urge to grab and take.

She finished bandaging, but didn't let go until she'd pressed her lips to each knuckle. "There." She glanced at him and blushed. "Sorry. I always liked the idea that kisses can heal." She dropped his hand and turned to face the faucet. "So you turned off the water below the sink first, is that right?"

Do that again. Kiss me—anywhere, anywhere at all. Just don't stop touching me. Making me feel alive again. He grabbed the coffee cup and sipped until his mind settled a bit. "Exactly. Otherwise you've got a hell of a mess to deal with." One deep breath, then another as he focused on the task at hand and not the woman beside him. "Sometimes in old houses, there's no cutoff below the sink, so you have to turn off the water either out front if there's a waterline, or where the water comes in from the well."

"What does Miss Margaret have?"

"*You* have a waterline out front," he reminded her.

Her brow furrowed a little. "It just doesn't seem real. I don't—I can't stay here. I have a life elsewhere." But something sad and uncertain fled over her features then. "Or I did, anyway." Her voice was so low, he wasn't sure he'd heard her right.

He waited for her to elaborate, but she didn't, and he couldn't afford to care. "So next you take off the handle." He handed her a screwdriver.

She took it hesitantly, then removed the screw that held the handle in place. She laid first the screw, then the handle on the counter in order. "Like this?"

"Exactly. Then you—" A cell phone rang at that moment, and she scanned the room, then went to pick it up from the kitchen table. When she looked at the display, she frowned. "I'm sorry. I have to take this." She put the screwdriver on the counter as she walked past him to the porch.

He watched her pace the boards, her expression by turns stormy and nervous. Her slender hands waved as she talked. At last she finished the call, flipped her phone closed and stood staring off the porch, her shoulders rounded.

He wasn't sure what to do, whether to finish the repair himself and leave, or wait and see if she wanted to talk.

He was certain, though, that he didn't like whatever had made her look so defeated.

At last she squared her shoulders and reentered.

"Problem?" he asked.

Her gaze snapped to his, the city lawyer replacing the woman who'd kissed his knuckles. "No big deal." She walked back to the sink, but he could see that her mind was elsewhere.

"I can finish this. You go take care of whatever you need to."

She flinched. "I can't, that's the problem." A distracted pause. Her fingers grasped the edge of the counter. "I can't fight shadows." She looked so sad for a second that he longed to draw her close and comfort her.

Him, a convicted felon. An accused second offender.

But maybe he was better than nothing. "I can listen, too, you know."

She bit at her lip as if deciding.

"Never mind." He turned back to his task.

"I…I made a mistake. Lost a big case, too, but that's the least of my troubles." When he glanced over, her expression was bleak. "My boss made me take time off. I'm an embarrassment to him, and he's up for reelection." She fell silent.

"So you should be back there defending your turf, that's what you're thinking?"

"Yes." She shrugged. "I don't know."

"You've worked hard to get there."

"How do you know that?"

"Even when you were being a rebel, you were a very determined one. You put everything into it."

A tiny smile curved her lips. "I guess I did." She shook her head. "I was such a mess. I ran away after my mother dragged me back home."

"You did?" He thought for a minute. "She didn't seem…Miss Margaret didn't think much of her."

"She was right not to."

"Where is your mother now?"

"I have no idea. I don't care. I've made my life."

Then, as if done with the topic, she turned toward the sink. "Show me the next step."

He hesitated. Wondered if he should probe further into her troubles. "You sure?"

"No, but I don't have any better ideas." She pointed at the faucet. "What comes off now?"

He understood this one thing: sometimes thinking about your problems could drive you crazy and didn't help one iota. Sometimes distractions were worth their weight in gold. "This is the stem," he said, noting a metal rod. "See that little piece of rubber at the base of it? That's called a washer."

Callie cast him a grateful glance, and they continued with the task at hand.

CHAPTER FOURTEEN

A REPORTER CALLED JOE, sniffing around, Anna had told Callie on the phone earlier. Joe Santiago was her section chief and mentor; he'd put himself at risk in his attempts to deflect the D.A.'s fury from her. Joe was the main reason she still had a job.

Anna hadn't needed to say what the reporter was trying to uncover. As Callie ripped at the vines she was trying to untangle from the gate at the Chambers house, she wondered if the leak had come from the defense counsel, who'd agreed not to press the issue in exchange for Callie being placed under supervision for the next year.

Of course, for all she knew, it could have been someone in her office. Her swift climb had created some enemies among those she'd leapfrogged, and to be frank, she'd been so focused on moving up that she'd left her share of bodies scattered in her wake.

"You ready?"

Startled, Callie looked up at Jessie Lee. "Ready?"

"For *Jeopardy*."

"What?"

"It's time to watch *Jeopardy*. On TV?" Jessie Lee's

tone was filled with the sort of patience one demon-
strates toward the clueless or infirm. "Granny insists."

Callie stared at her. "Go right ahead. I'm not done."
She gestured toward the back gate.

"You have to come, too. Everybody does."

"That's nonsense. David won't—" Callie's voice
died off as she witnessed the same man descending the
ladder from the roof he'd been repairing.

"I told you." Jessie Lee's grin was unrepentant. "Now
get a move on." She grabbed Callie's hand and all but
dragged her inside.

David reached the back door before they did, and
held the screen door open for them. "Ladies."

Callie slowed and let Jessie Lee precede her. "Is this
for real?" She kept her voice low.

His eyes crinkled at the corners. "You better believe
it. As far as Granny Chambers is concerned, the world
stops for Alex Trebek." He bent nearer. "Just between
us, I think she's got a crush on him."

"But…we have a list."

"You've been working hard all day." He glanced
down at her hands and frowned. "Your skin is scraped."
He turned one of them over, then the second. "And
you've got blisters. Where are your gloves?"

"They keep falling off. It's no big deal."

"Yes, it is. You have lady hands." He towed her
inside. "Stay right there." He pointed to the sink. "Jessie
Lee," he called out. When the girl arrived, her impatient
glance dissolved when she heard what he needed, and
she raced off.

Callie joined him in the doorway. "Just let this be," she hissed. "I'm fine."

"You're lucky you haven't touched poison ivy," he shot back.

"Hush up now, you two," Granny ordered. "What is China?" she said to the screen. When the contestant echoed her, she socked a fist in the air.

"John Wayne attended USC on what kind of scholarship?" asked Trebek.

"What is football?" Granny craned her head toward David, brows lifted.

He nodded just as the contestant echoed her.

Granny's grin was wide.

"The Greek word beginning with *H* that means unwarranted pride."

Callie looked over at him, but his eyes were focused on the screen.

Granny shrugged. "What is *hubris?*" David prompted.

"Huh," she responded, but quickly switched her gaze to the television.

Jessie Lee skidded to a stop before them. "Here." She thrust the contents she held into David's hands.

"Thanks, Jessie Lee." He began bandaging.

"Science for one hundred," said the contestant.

"The science of raising food or animals," intoned the host.

"What is husbandry?" David answered softly at the same moment Granny crowed it.

Callie would only have been right on one of those three, but as the show continued, he never missed. The topics ranged from seventeenth-century art to chemistry. She even got into the spirit of things, surprised to be having fun when most of her answers were wrong.

Once she and David had experienced joy, had teased and laughed with innocent exuberance, full of life and the high of being young.

She'd forgotten what that felt like.

She mused over the inconsistencies in him, a convicted felon reviled by most of the town yet capable of such kindness, clearly self-educated far beyond the high school graduation he'd missed. The cynical prosecutor in her would have dismissed the last few days as an aberration, a con job.

But as he gently cleaned and doctored her hands, his touch light but reassuring, his nearness a beacon of both sensual promise and comforting strength, Callie's thoughts tumbled like a child's unsteady tower of blocks.

Her fingers jerked in response to the tumult in her mind.

"Sorry," he said unevenly. "I didn't mean to hurt you. I'm almost done."

You didn't hurt me, she nearly protested, but in her confusion, she instead remained silent until he was done. Her brain was exploding with too much input: questions about David, worries about her job, conflicted feelings about Oak Hollow and the unwanted responsibilities that had been dumped on her by a woman she owed a lot to.

The second that David was finished, despite *Jeopardy* not being over, she didn't return with him to the living room but instead escaped outside and put away her tools.

She was sorry to leave the respite of a lighter atmosphere, of time spent with a man who brought back the boy. She couldn't afford it, though; she had to figure out how to deal with the reporter, had to plan her next step in the quest to regain her reputation, how to extricate herself from Oak Hollow without hurting anyone. She couldn't seem to think straight around David. They were all but done with the list. She'd walk home and use the time to get her head on straight.

DAVID STAYED until the game show was over a few minutes later, when he discovered that Callie wasn't with them anymore and must have gone outside. He followed and began piling the vines Callie had cleared, along with the rotten shingles he'd replaced on the roof. The shadows were lengthening, and they needed to finish up. He had a debt to pay off, however unsettling it was to spend time in Callie's presence, and only plowing through the list would accomplish that.

By the time he'd carried his last load, he still hadn't seen her. She hadn't said a word after his clumsy bandaging job. Had he hurt her that much? He was no nurse and never professed to be, but he'd apologized, hadn't he? There was no reason for her to just take off like that. Now he had to find her and apologize again, he guessed, yet what the hell else could he say but—

He went stock-still. Her clippers were gone.

And, he realized, so was she.

Damn it. She'd come to the house with him, so she would be on foot. The shadows lengthened quickly in the mountains as evening approached. She'd be out there alone, dressed in that tight T-shirt and jeans practically painted on her legs, every curve and half her naked flesh on display with God knows who driving by—

"Jessie Lee!" he bellowed.

The girl poked her head out. "You two want to stay for supper?"

"She's gone. I'm not sure she knows her way from here. Tell Granny I'll be back in the morning to clean this up before I start again. I'll just put the rest of the tools up in the shed—"

"Let me," Jessie Lee said, sprinting toward him. "I'll take care of it. You go rescue the city slicker."

"You sure?"

She nodded.

"Thanks. And tell Granny I appreciate the invitation."

He charged toward the piece of junk he was driving. He needed time—and funds—to do an engine overhaul, but for now he held his breath until the vehicle started, then took off in the direction he hoped she'd gone.

As SHE WALKED, Callie's mind was filled with images and questions. Why would Anna call her with that veiled warning? Anna got along much better with Leslie Carlson, the other attorney who shared Anna's services, and Callie and Leslie were not friends, never had been. Both were too competitive. Was this a ploy on Leslie's part to frighten her into coming back before the D.A. was ready for her to? But if Callie stayed in Nowheresville, she left others in her office a clear field. Out of sight, out of mind.

The D.A. had refrained from firing her only because of her record, which up to then had been sterling. *You're the brightest lawyer on my staff, Callie. What were you thinking, withholding critical information? The sky was the limit for you, and now I've got a judge raising hell over your behavior. I've admired your guts in the past, but you went too far. You'd better thank your lucky stars for that not-guilty verdict or you'd be out on the street already.*

Gerald had taken steps to keep Callie's screw up quiet, but if she became an open liability, he'd have no choice but to fire her. In addition, she'd lost a high-profile case, which reflected badly on him. So when Gerald had forced a vacation on her in lieu of a suspension, she knew he'd gone as far as he could for her. If she showed up at the office now, especially with a reporter sniffing around, she risked losing everything.

But the wolves were nipping at her heels, and staying away allowed the rumor mill to continue to grind. You were only as good as your last conviction, and others would view her continued absence as confirmation of her guilt, along with a healthy dose of cowardice.

Stay away. Go back. The defendant had been guilty, no matter that her witness had been seeking to exact her own revenge for his earlier rape and beating of her. That didn't change the fact of his guilt, but one overzealous cop's behavior during the arrest had gotten crucial evidence of the recent crime excluded from testimony. Without it, the defendant would go on to do more violence, so Callie had made her choice not to reveal the witness's ulterior motive once she learned of it. Now the defendant was free, and Callie's efforts to stop him were all for naught.

"Well, lookee here, Stanley," came a voice that chilled her.

Her head whipped around to see a huge pickup roll up beside her. She'd been so lost in her thoughts she hadn't heard the bass rumble of its motor. Although the passenger window was down, in the dimming light she couldn't make out the face.

There were no houses nearby, no place to run. Callie stood her ground. She'd dealt with thugs before.

"I do believe we got us the outlander who thought it was one hell of an idea to let that murdering son of a bitch out of jail." The speaker leaned closer, and she recognized him then.

Mickey Patton.

Showing fear was the worst thing you could do with a predator, she'd learned.

She wasn't in a position of power now, however, and in the animal kingdom, confrontation could escalate to violence. She had to tread carefully.

"Got nothin' to say for yourself, girl? Why don't you invite the lady to join us, Stanley?" *Lady* was said with a sneer. "It's gettin' dark out here, sugar. We'd best give you a ride to town."

"I'm fine, thank you," she managed. "I'm out for the exercise."

"Oh, you don't need to worry about your girlish figure. Looks mighty fine to me." His voice was oily, and even if his eyes weren't clearly visible, she could feel them run over her body like an unseen hand. She shivered in disgust. She'd been around too many men like this, men who treated women as less than human to feel superior when they were the pathetic ones.

But pathetic didn't mean not dangerous. She cursed herself for being too casual, for treating Oak Hollow like Mayberry. In her job, she dressed in clothing that never incited and clearly said *Do not take me lightly.* Yet here she was, on a deserted road with nothing but her wits to protect her.

"I'd get out, but I'm still recuperatin' from that bastard tryin' to kill me, see. Stanley, get your ass out of the truck and help the lady inside."

"Mickey, I don't think…"

An ally, however unwilling. Callie's attention was caught on the driver. "No need. I'm visiting Mrs. Chambers, and it's about time for dinner." She turned around. Granny's was close.

"I didn't ask what you think, Stanley, now did I? Move it."

"Mickey…"

"Goddammit!"

She saw Mickey start to open the passenger door, injured or not, and she knew her time was up. She took off running toward Granny's and heard him bellowing. Waited for the truck to come after her and tried not to panic.

A car appeared over the rise ahead, and she tensed.

Then she realized it was David and nearly collapsed from relief. Thank God.

David slammed on the brakes, leaped from his vehicle. "What's wrong?" But at that same instant, his attention snagged on the man emerging from the pickup. His expression hardened to stone. "Get in the car." He started forward.

"Oh, yeah, come on," taunted Patton.

"David, no!" She reversed course and threw herself in his path, lowering her voice. "You can't. If you touch him, you'll be back in jail."

"You always do what she tells you, Davey boy?" Patton's mocking singsong was like a red cape to a bull. "My, my…guess you best be real careful, like she says. You sure wouldn't want to wind up back in Jackson sooner. 'Course you'll be there anyway, so what's the difference?"

David brushed right past her.

She wheeled to put herself in his way again. It was like standing in front of a freight train at full speed. "David, please!" There was no way to do this with subtlety, not now, so she put both her hands on his chest, desperate to distract him. "I'm all right. He didn't hurt me. Take me back, please. David—"

His focus snapped to her, but the man she saw was half-mad. Logic would make no impression. His eyes burned, and his entire body was rigid with fury, nearly shaking with the power of his craving to do damage to the man taunting him from the safety of his status as victim.

Looking at him now, anyone would wonder how David could be innocent of the assault. If she hadn't known other facets of him, she'd judge him guilty as charged.

But she did know those other Davids. "Please," she begged. "Think about your mother. It will kill her for you to go to jail again." Her fingers were wrapped around his rigid biceps, barely covering half the circumference as she sought to hold him back. She lowered her voice. "It'll kill you, too." She took a deep breath. "And I couldn't stand it, either," she admitted. "Please, David."

His glare radiated loathing and a brittle rage, knowing she was right but hating it to his core.

Being the agent of his misery ate at her.

"Stanley, if you want your friend in one piece, I'd suggest you get him out of here now," she called, never removing her eyes from David's.

"Come on, Mickey. You've had your fun," said Stanley. "He could beat the living hell out of you, and you're in no condition to fight back. Let's just go."

The silence that ensued rang with violence teetering on the edge of exploding.

"Piece of shit." Patton spit on the ground. "Hide behind a woman's skirts, you goddamn coward."

David's entire frame reacted. His muscles readied for the charge.

As he initiated that first step, Callie did the only thing she could think of to stop him: she fell back as though he'd knocked her down.

Her fall snapped his fixation on Patton. When he looked down in alarm, she saw the anger recede a fraction.

"Bring it on, you son of a—" shouted Patton.

But Stanley hit the gas and the pickup roared off.

David lifted her to her feet, the movements lacking his usual powerful grace. Rage still enveloped him like a poisonous cloud. He set her aside quickly. "Get in the car."

"David, I know I caused—"

"Get in the goddamn car!" He rounded the hood without looking back.

SMOTHERING SILENCE FILLED the interior of the vehicle as he drove them toward Miss Margaret's. Callie sat like a penitent child, twisting her fingers in her lap.

The very idea of apologizing for keeping him out of jail—out of *prison* for the rest of his life, curse him—rapidly frayed the reins on her own temper. Another assault charge would make his conviction on the first much too easy for the prosecution, even if he wasn't already stonewalling all efforts toward his defense. She opened her mouth to point out that he was wrong to be angry at her. But she subsided. He wasn't wrong, not really. He'd been put in a bad position because she'd taken off on her own, near dark, in a strange place. Without him... She shuddered, contemplating what could have happened to her, had she been forced into that pickup.

Her ire receded, replaced by chagrin. Just then, he pulled into Miss Margaret's driveway and shut off the engine, then emerged and rounded the hood.

"David," she began, "Listen—"

Her next words vanished as she was bodily lifted to her feet. "Damn it, Callie." He crushed her into his embrace. "You could have been—" His voice was low and rough and haunted as he wrapped her more tightly in his arms.

For a moment she simply stood there, catching up, relishing the feeling of safety, soaking in the warmth, the sense of being protected from all harm. It was a novel experience for Lady Justice, one she'd assumed she was too tough to need.

She'd been wrong. He was here, in that second, *David*. Her David, the one she'd loved with all her young girl's heart. The David who'd taken her side against everyone in his life, who'd risked everything and lost big, thanks solely to her. Yet never once, no matter how many people sought to make him see sense, had he deserted her or their baby. That precious little life that never had a chance.

The tears that Callie thought she'd buried beyond retrieval rose in a scalding gush, bathing her heart in acid, blistering her lungs and spilling out to wet David's shirt. She wept and wept, digging her fingers into the long muscles of his back and clinging as she had never allowed herself to do to one single soul since the day she'd left this place.

"I'm sorry, I'm so sorry for everything…" Suddenly she sagged beneath the crushing load of her misery.

David picked her up as though she weighed nothing. He crossed the grass and stepped onto the front porch, then settled in the old swing and began to rock her as she cried.

"It's all my fault. If I'd left you alone, you'd never have had to go through any of this."

"Shh," he soothed, and bundled her closer. He tipped her head back and stared into her eyes. After precious, crystalline seconds, he touched his mouth to hers.

The kiss was gentle, a butterfly's wing against first

her lower lip, then the upper one. A sweet benediction, a pardon. "Callie…" His voice, husky and tender, skimmed her ragged heart, drifted over her skin, tugged low in her belly.

This David, the real David, could lift her misery, had always made her feel like someone who was worthy, someone different from Callie the neglected child, the unwanted one still so very much alive inside her. She'd clawed and climbed, achieved and won, but all of it was on the back of that girl she'd tried so hard to leave behind. To bury.

David's hands began to move, and his mouth tantalized, his touch a healing. He was the only link to that rebellious girl who'd simply wanted to be loved, she understood now.

For a few bittersweet months, she had been. They had been young and naive, yes, but their bond had been real.

How had she not recognized that she had not been whole since the day they'd been parted? That locking the past away could not work forever? She yearned to open her chest and let the sweet succor pour in to wash away all the pain of the past. Longed to do the same for him.

She could, she realized, do that now, at this instant. Or she could at least try to hope her touch had the same effect on him.

Callie sat up on his lap.

David's eyes were both clouded and wary.

"Shh…close your eyes."

He stared. Frowned. Then to her surprise, after a moment, he complied.

She began with his hair, stroking over it, tunneling her fingers into the thick chestnut mass, then rubbing his scalp in slow circles.

David groaned, and she felt his big body relent a little. He looked so weary, as though he'd carried a very heavy burden for a long, long time. "Lean on me," she murmured. When he stiffened slightly at the notion, she kept the slow strokes going. "Just for now, let me take care of you." When at last his head lowered a little, she brought his forehead to rest against her chest, then lengthened her caresses to move over those powerful shoulders.

David wondered where she was going with this, but it felt so good, he wasn't sure he cared. Moment by moment, inch by inch, she was unknotting nerves tangled by the fight to survive the past fifteen years. The last three months of being a pariah.

He realized that he had not fully relaxed since the day he'd stood over Ned Compton's body…or for many months before that actually, as he'd struggled to protect his mother from the abuse no one but him had suspected.

Callie's gentle fingers returned to his face, tracing his forehead, his cheekbones, his jaw. If there was an instant of panic over not remaining alert, she soon dispelled it with the magic of her hands. With the kisses she pressed to his eyelids, his face…his throat.

Her tongue slicked a trail down to his collarbone, and he groaned aloud. She had no idea what she was doing to him.

His body responded immediately, vividly.

Or perhaps she did know.

He'd never felt this layering of sensations, of easing and soothing. Of tantalizing temptation.

She smoothed her hands over his shoulders, kneading the tense muscles, tracing circles on his chest. Her fingers skimmed down his T-shirt and began to lift it.

If she couldn't feel that reaction…

Her flesh touched his as she bared him. She set her teeth to his throat and nipped.

He ignited like a torch. Grabbed her hips and surged to his feet, wrapping her legs around his waist.

And bolted for the door.

Callie gasped but never paused in covering his face with kisses, letting her hands roam. She stripped off his T-shirt. He struggled to get them inside the house and to the bed before they tumbled in a heap to the floor and he took her right where they lay.

There were about a hundred reasons why they shouldn't be doing this, why he should drop her right there and run as fast as his legs would carry him, away from her.

But there was one reason he would not, could not.

That reason was Callie.

If hell itself reached up to drag him into the fiery pit, then that's just what would have to happen. She was here with him at last. They'd never had a chance to truly be together without sneaking around, with only their two bodies glorying in each other as he'd sensed they could one day—when she wasn't lost and fourteen pretending to be older and he wasn't wrestling with a whole town's aspirations.

When they were only Callie, only David…who might have made a life together, if so much else hadn't intervened.

So he laid her gently on the bed, and he looked at her in the moonlight.

"A real mattress," she marveled, and smiled. "Imagine."

She sprawled there, all moon-silvered curves and magic, and held her arms out to him. He wanted to join her more than anything in his life, but—

"Stop thinking," she whispered. "We both do too much of that." She rose to sitting and reached for his belt buckle.

If she opened the buttons of his jeans now, this would all be over in seconds. "Uh-uh." He grasped her wrists and lifted them above her head while pressing her back into the sheets and letting his mouth do the talking for him.

Soon she was squirming and sighing and driving him half out of his mind, but he was determined not to stop until she'd gone crazy right along with him. He teased and tormented, each caress torturing him as much as her.

Then her hands slipped loose and she tried to unseat him and reverse their positions.

He shook his head. "Not yet, Callie. Please let me do this. Let me have you." With an uncertain smile and hope in her eyes, she relented.

So he ruthlessly restrained the ache of craving to drive himself into her and instead focused on the tenderness he sensed she needed. With his body, with his lips and hands, he paid homage to the woman she'd created out of a small, wounded girl.

And when he set his mouth to the heart of her and heard her gasp, then moan, a warm flame lit within him, the first spark of light in a long darkness.

Truth to tell, she probably had more experience in lovemaking than he did. He'd gone from being a grieving teenage father to the brutality of prison, and he'd only been with one woman, one time, since his release. He wasn't completely sure he was doing this right, at least until he felt her body gather, registered the trembling in her legs, sensed the power growing within her at each touch of his tongue, each caress of his lips…

"David—" Callie gasped. Came apart in his arms. She gripped him fiercely as she flew, then melted like butter. In the moonlight slanting across the bed, her mouth curved in a beautiful, very satisfied smile.

Though his own body burned to join her, still his heart warmed at the sight of her. He smiled back.

After a moment, she pounced. Toppled him to his back and began to torture him again. He was ready, so ready—

Then, with a sinking heart, he realized he couldn't let her and imprisoned her hands to stop her. "I'm fine."

Her eyes went dark with hurt. "You're not. Why would—"

He'd never imagined he could still blush, not after all he'd been through in his life, but a mingle of shame and embarrassment burned his cheeks. "I just—I don't have anything to protect you. I didn't—I never expected…"

If Callie had ever doubted that she could still love him, this moment would have ended that concern. She tangled her fingers in his and bent to him, unable to stem her smile. "No modern woman of a certain age group," she murmured just above his lips, "even one with a social life as pathetic as mine, goes anywhere without condoms in her purse." Then she swiped her tongue over the seam of his lips. "Wait right here, big guy." She leaped from the bed and was back in seconds, brandishing them with triumph.

"Now," she said, and grinned, waggling her eyebrows at him, "Just lie back and think of England."

When he laughed, she thought she'd never heard anything sweeter. Laughter had been scarce in their time together, both years ago and certainly since she'd returned.

But I refuse to think about the real world tonight. Instead, she tossed the condoms on the bed and dove at him.

At first they played, then Callie, still tingling from the bliss he'd given her, attempted to do the same for him and draw out this unspeakable pleasure.

But if she'd thought to control the pace, she'd been wrong. All too soon, David, bared under her touch and breathtaking to behold, took charge again. "This is going to be too quick," he warned. "But I'll make it up to you, I promise."

"I think you already did," she said on a moan.

"I barely got started," he vowed. He took her soaring again. Gave her rapture, but gave her something more.

Hope. Sweetness. Much lay ahead for them to battle, but they would triumph, together this time, she was determined. United once more, only this time she was no scared teen.

But all of that was for later.

For now, David's lean, hard body filled her, thrilled her…rocketed her back to bliss. The power of the man, the joining…together, they were so much more than when apart. She'd often derided the notion of a magical click.

Until, as they clung to each other in the aftermath, she felt it.

Now she understood how badly she'd needed to experience the bond. Abject terror gripped her at the prospect of having this precious unity torn from her again. Callie closed her eyes and forced herself to calm. There was so little she could control right now, but she could be in command of her reaction.

Resolutely she cleared her mind of fears that would wreck the beauty of this moment, this man. Instead, she cradled his head where he lay heavily against her breast. "I love you," she murmured softly.

For one priceless second, she thought she felt his arms tighten back.

But he said nothing, and she said no more.

Soon slumber claimed them both.

CHAPTER FIFTEEN

DAVID WOKE before dawn. Someone was too close to him. Instantly the old prison reflexes kicked in. He braced to defend himself.

Then he heard soft breathing and remembered.

Callie. Oh, sweet heaven, Callie. The night and its glory swooped in, obliterating every other thought in a rush of overpowering tenderness and sharp, aching need.

He turned his head and saw her blond curls against his bicep as she cuddled into his side. One slender, pale hand lay over his skin bronzed from spending every possible second outside. He'd thought the freedom to be out in the air, to move in any direction he chose, was the sweetest blessing of his release.

Until this moment, it had been.

But now there was Callie.

Going back in a cage would kill him. He'd believed that to be the worst fate possible, but suddenly there was something even more devastating.

Walking away from her now.

But he had to. There was no win for him, no matter what she might believe. She didn't know the whole story, and he couldn't tell her.

And that story was all that could save him.

For a second, David let himself contemplate options he had never countenanced before. He could go now, today, make his way out of the country by whatever means necessary. He was strong, he could work, he could make money to send to his mother secretly and to repay Callie for the bail she had posted.

Maybe Callie would even join him. They could start all over. Create the life they had begun to imagine as teenagers. They were older now, but still young enough to have a rich, full life.

Mexico. The Caribbean. Callie had no roots, no one to belong to. Maybe she would. Maybe…

Who was he kidding? She was an officer of the court, a prosecutor. She actually believed in the system that had nearly destroyed him. She would want him to stay, to fix this mess with Patton. To fight for him, even though doing so would cost her. David didn't know exactly what she faced back in Philadelphia, but he had a strong sense that she couldn't afford to ally her cause with his.

He had a past he couldn't reveal and a future that was untenable. His mother was rooted in Oak Hollow, and taking her away would kill her. Even if a miracle happened and he was cleared this time, the town was full of Mickey Pattons who would never forgive him for the death of Ned Compton.

Circles, always circles leading right back to one fateful night, one life-altering decision he would not change even if he could.

Callie sighed in her sleep. David rose on one elbow

to peer down at her, wishing he could afford to touch her, taste her, love her again and again. He would never tire of her. Never get his fill.

Never have the words to tell her what this night had meant, even if he had the luxury of waiting for her to awaken.

With regret and longing weighing down his heart, David rolled as quietly as he could manage and slipped from Callie's bed.

They could never repeat this. Somehow he had to make her leave, return to her life, save her career.

She could be saved. He could not.

And he refused to see her go down with him.

I love you, he said silently as he stood over her, scanning her features once more while his heart ached.

Then he slipped on his clothes and stole into the night.

HE DROVE AWAY as quietly as possible, and headed to his mother's. The more he considered his situation, the more he was certain that he must disappear. Callie would never give up unless he forced her away. Made her hate him.

Believing he had jumped bail would make him guilty in everyone's eyes, maybe even hers. Taking her money and leaving her high and dry ought to do the trick. She didn't have to know that he would repay her if it took the rest of his life. Just getting her out of Oak Hollow and safe again was all that mattered now.

His mother would understand, and he'd take care of her, too.

Feeling a little more settled, he turned down the lane that led to his mother's house, preoccupied with the logistics of where to go next and what to take.

Too late, he saw Sheriff Carver's car waiting for him.

Desperation nearly got the better of him, urging him to throw the car in Reverse and race from the sick feeling in the pit of his stomach, even though this vehicle was nowhere near being up to a chase.

It was also his mother's only transportation, which she would need once he was back in jail.

The sheriff stared at him as though he could read the temptation on David's face.

David shut off the car and got out. Stood in silence.

The man, another of Ned Compton's very close friends, surveyed him with contempt. Finally he spoke. "I have to ask you to come with me, Langley."

"What for?"

"Got to ask you some questions about where you were last night."

"What's wrong with asking me here?"

One eyebrow arched. "'Cause the judge will likely be wanting to hear what you have to say. Might as well do it all at once."

"Am I under arrest?"

"Not yet," the sheriff responded. "Remains to be determined. Your mama tells me she hasn't seen you since yesterday afternoon. Where you been, boy?"

David spotted his mother standing white-faced and frozen in the doorway. "Don't you involve her in this."

The man's eyes narrowed. "You trying to tell me

how to do my job? You want to make this hard, son, things can go south pretty quick. I believe I just might have probable cause to arrest you again, unless you've got information that would change my mind."

If she were here, Callie would be raising Cain about asking for his lawyer, but she wasn't. Though backing off stuck in his craw, he didn't want his mother exposed to any more violence. "I'm not after any trouble."

"Then you best start telling me what I want to know. Otherwise I just might decide to hold you until we can set up a hearing with the judge. You don't want that, you talk to me."

David gritted his teeth. "What do you want to know?"

"Where you were last night, for starters."

"Why?"

"I'm asking the questions, boy. Where have you been?"

"You tell me first what's going on." Had Patton said something? David didn't want to be the first to bring up the altercation with Callie yesterday, but he couldn't imagine what else this could be about. If that was the case, his only defense was Callie. He wouldn't let her be dragged into this. "I think I'd better have my attorney present."

"Fine." The sheriff grabbed his elbow.

David couldn't help tensing, pulling back.

The man's eyes lit. "Now you've done it. Consider yourself under arrest. You have the right to remain silent…"

A pure animal instinct shot through him, the urge to

fight or run screaming in his head. He could not go back. Could not be locked up again.

"David!" his mother cried out.

Mindful of her, he brutally reined in the impulse to fight being shoved toward the sheriff's vehicle.

"What's happening? What shall I do?" she pleaded.

"Nothing, Mom." He clawed for a hold on his composure. "I'll be fine. Just go inside. I'll be back soon." He knew he was lying. It was all over for him. He settled into a leaden resignation.

The only alternative was to lose his mind.

But as the car pulled away, he heard his mother's piteous cries. Saw her stagger, then run after them in a halting gait, her robe flapping loose as she clutched it in one hand. "Leave him alone!"

The sound of her terror was all he could hear as they drove off.

CALLIE STIRRED and blinked as sunlight slapped her eyes.

Her lids flew wide, as memory flared in her brain, and one palm covered her chest while the heartbeat beneath accelerated.

Cautiously she glanced to the left.

No one. Maybe she'd dreamed him.

Delicious soreness in her body said otherwise. David had been here, really here, right beside her in Miss Margaret's bed. Perhaps she should feel odd about all they'd done in the darkness where a sweet old woman had slept. But she didn't. Callie grinned. She was almost certain Miss Margaret would approve. The older woman had liked David back then and apparently had still believed in him until she died. Miss Margaret's own love affair had been cut short by tragedy, but maybe Callie and David could close the circle for her.

Oh, good grief, her common sense intruded. *You don't live here, and how are you going to explain being involved with an ex-con to your boss?* Especially, she sobered, when he was going to trial again.

The night's magic soured under the harsh light of truth. *It was just good sex,* a part of her lectured.

No…it was great sex. Amazing, mind-bending stuff. *Let the record so state, Your Honor. The man turned me inside out…and I'm pretty sure I did the same to him.*

But her heart twisted with a longing that wouldn't die. It had been more, whatever this was between them. There was a tender lining beneath the heat.

So where was he? She glanced around and noticed his clothes were missing. She shouldn't be surprised, she guessed, but she would have liked to wake up with him. Maybe make love again.

For a moment she lost herself in reminiscing. A sweet shiver ran through her.

Someone banged hard on the front door. "Callie, come quick!"

Callie sat up. "Jessie Lee?"

"They've got him, Callie. The sheriff has David."

"What?" She couldn't be hearing right. Callie leaped from the mattress and searched frantically for a robe. "Hold on, I'm coming!" she called.

Breathless, she raced to the front door and opened it.

Jessie Lee appeared terrified. "They came for him this morning. Took him back to jail."

"For what?" She gripped Jessie Lee's shoulders. "How do you know this?"

"Granny saw the sheriff go by with David in the back seat. She called David's mom, but she was so scared she was hard to understand. I just took off, I didn't wait for them to finish. I'm not sure what's going on, but I knew you could fix it."

Dear God. Had Patton filed a complaint? That bastard. "I'll get dressed. You call Granny and find out exactly what Mrs. Langley said to her."

"Want me to make you some coffee? I know how," Jessie Lee said.

Callie didn't really want to wait for it to drip, but she needed her mind sharp, so she nodded. "Just one cup is plenty." That would go fairly quickly. "Thank you, Jessie Lee."

"He's gonna be all right, isn't he, Callie?"

"Absolutely." She repressed a shiver of foreboding. Reminded herself that this had to be about Patton, didn't it? So all she had to do was tell what really happened, and David would be okay.

But she couldn't legally defend him, and being a witness complicated things. To say nothing of what would happen if anyone knew where he'd spent the night.

She turned back. "Jessie Lee?"

"Yes, ma'am?"

"Let me use the phone first." She'd better have David's attorney there right away, since she wasn't sure exactly what was going on. Capwell might be over-loaded, but she would get him to David quickly if she had to drag him there herself.

She started dialing. While she waited for the phone to ring, she mourned the loss of the night, the hope, the promise.

But she was not going down without a fight. This was wrong, and she had to fix it.

"YOU CAN'T SEE HIM," said the deputy at the door.

"What?"

"Langley already told the sheriff he didn't want you involved in his case."

"Are you kidding me? Look, his attorney is out of town, and he needs legal counsel." She tried to shove past. "Let me talk to him."

The burly deputy stepped into her path. "I'm telling you he was real clear about it. He knows his attorney isn't coming, but he still doesn't want to see you."

The words were a knife to the heart. Even before last night's magic, they would have hurt, but she'd thought…

"He said to tell you last night was fun, but it's over." The deputy's leer ended on a faint snicker.

What? Callie reeled. He'd *told* them? He put what had meant everything to her up for ridicule? She faltered under the shock of it. Last night had been…everything.

To her, at least. Apparently not to…

Stunned and disbelieving, she turned away from the avid gaze peering past her defenses and into her wounded heart.

No. David wouldn't do this. His eyes had been soft and open, wounded and weary. He'd needed her as much as—

He'd been gone this morning. Without a word. And now…

"I want to speak with the sheriff, then."

The deputy looked at her then with something that might have been pity. "Sorry, ma'am, but he ain't here right now."

"Why has David been taken into custody? On what grounds?"

"Ma'am, there ain't nothing you can do here. I don't have to tell you that." Then he seemed to consider. "Look, there was a complaint filed. Another assault. Can't just let this man walk around free to attack ordinary citizens."

Ordinary citizens. Mickey Patton was anything but that, and Callie had no more doubts that's who had filed the false claim. "I may be able to shed light on the charge. I'll just wait here for the sheriff."

"He won't be back until tomorrow. Had to attend a funeral."

She started to open her mouth to insist that the deputy take her statement.

He said to tell you last night was fun, but it's over.

David couldn't be clearer that he didn't want her help.

Last night must have been the aberration.

She couldn't think about last night, not and keep her composure. She walked away with all the dignity she could muster, moving as rapidly as her weak knees would carry her to her car. Somehow she inserted the key, turned the ignition, drove away…

She saw nothing, only an endless desert before her as she drove back through the mountains to Oak Hollow.

He'd talked to virtual strangers about them. Exposed her. Made her a fool.

She was tired of fighting him. He'd told her again and again to leave him alone; it was time to listen. She would pack. Miss Margaret's ridiculous thirty days could rot in hell. What did Callie care for any of these people who had never cared one whit about her? She could support herself, and whatever became of the property was no concern of hers….

She barely made it into the driveway at her great-aunt's before she dropped her head to the steering wheel and allowed the searing pain to take over.

Last night was a lie. Her hopes—absurd, girlish dreams—were ashes. More, they were the worst kind of self-deception. David didn't love her, had never loved her. She'd had some great sex and sold herself a fantasy of whopper proportions.

Well, enough of that. Callie straightened in the seat. Screw David and screw Oak Hollow; she would be just fine without either one. She didn't need anyone, not now, not ever.

She shoved open the car door, grabbed her purse and stalked toward the house, every tap of her heels a drumbeat of fury displacing naked pain.

I will not cry over you, David Langley, not ever again, you hear me?

Anger felt better, a familiar friend. Anger had propelled her through college and law school, kept her awake through countless nights of studying dry texts as she marched her way from a past filled with defeat and into a future where she was a winner.

She would win again.

Callie climbed up the porch steps, with a lighter tread, strengthened by resolve never to open herself to such misery again. She'd had to go through this, she rationalized, to be done with the unresolved feelings of the past.

She would give her statement to David's attorney, but she was done with him and with the past. She had a future to secure, and her job was all she had. She reached for the screen door handle, already preparing a mental packing list—

An envelope fell to the ground when the screen door opened.

Callie Hunter—IMPORTANT, was handwritten on the front.

Frowning, she slit the envelope open with her fingers as she shouldered her way inside. A single sheet of paper lay within. She drew it out and unfolded it.

Only one sentence in nondescript block print:

Ned Compton is the key.

What did that mean? Who would have sent this?

Her fury stalled in its tracks. Her attention captured, she sank to the arm of the sofa and puzzled over the intent of the sender…and who might care enough about David to intervene.

Something wasn't right, and she realized abruptly just how distracted she'd been by Miss Margaret's bequest, by her worries over her job, her uncharacteristic confusion over how to proceed. By, above all, David himself, his overpowering physical presence and the cloud of emotion that accompanied their past.

She thought back to her shock at the astonishing reversal in David's trajectory, how the star athlete and talented student had become a killer when nothing in his life predicted a fate even close to that. Sure, there were the cases of "I never would have suspected" when neighbors or coworkers reported some heinous crime, but all that she knew about the makings of a criminal argued against it ever happening to David. Generally the signs were there if you knew where to look.

There were also the discrepancies in the present: how he cared for his mother, the good he'd done for Jessie Lee, the respect he'd shown Granny's *Jeopardy* addiction…the beautiful carving at their baby's grave.

Something indeed was wrong with this picture.

Including David's actions of the morning, if she could manage to get her hurt feelings out of the way. He was a protector, she'd known since she met him.

Could it be that he was protecting her now?

Or was she simply so desperate not to be made a fool of after she'd lost her heart again last night that she was grasping at straws?

Ned Compton is the key.

She'd asked a lot of questions about David, she realized, as she'd talked to people in the community. But she'd given short shrift to one essential aspect of investigating a crime: learning as much about the victim as about the alleged perpetrator.

Ned Compton had many friends in Oak Hollow, but none of them had resided with him. None might know him the way the two people who'd lived with him did.

David had been clear that he didn't want her anywhere near him, and she could only speculate at this point about why. If he was refusing to speak with her, then she would go to the next person on her list.

David's mother.

Ned Compton's widow.

CHAPTER SIXTEEN

"SHE SAYS she's not leaving until you see her." The deputy flipped an opened envelope through the bars, where it landed on the floor. "She said maybe this would change your mind."

David remained on the cot and stared at the paper, its ragged edges symbolizing the complete destruction of any control he might have had over his life. No privacy, not even the most basic courtesy. He was held in contempt by his jailers and by the townspeople with a few rare exceptions. He had no future here, and the sheriff had made it very clear that Mickey Patton's word would be believed over anything David could produce, short of a videotape of the confrontation, which David had yet to explain.

The sheriff, he reminded himself, had been a deputy when Ned Compton died and had made no bones about his glee when David went to jail.

All David had on his side was Callie, stubborn, loyal Callie. He appreciated her defense of him more than he could afford to let her know, but how long would her faith in him hold with her job in jeopardy, with no more chances for them to be together outside an interview room? He didn't kid himself that he would ever get out of jail again.

Not unless he was willing to tell the truth, which he could never do.

"Well? You gonna read it or not?"

He eyed the envelope again. "Since you've obviously done so, why don't you just tell me what it says?"

"Read it yourself. Don't make sense anyway."

Why hadn't David's callous words sent Callie running? Why wouldn't she give up on him?

Because she's got the heart of a lion, that's why.

David sighed and reached for the paper on the floor, holding it in his hand for a moment before reluctantly sliding it from the envelope. Slowly he unfolded the single sheet.

You have to see me. For the sake of one lost angel, if nothing else.

He bowed his head. *Not fair, Callie. Not even a little fair.*

Damn it. What could she have to say but what he'd already heard? If she understood the true situation…

But she didn't. Couldn't, as long as he continued to lie to her.

There's no hope, can't you see that? You're wasting your time. Go back to Philadelphia and get on with your life.

His own was over. Any hope for them had fled.

But one stubborn little seed pushed its fragile stem up from the depths of darkness. Up through a tiny crack in the grimy asphalt that was his life. Maybe she knew something…this was her arena after all. Maybe…

"Damn you, Callie," he muttered, but there was little heat in it.

"All right," he said to the deputy. "I'll see her." He refused to dwell on whether the appeal was simply having one last chance to be near her.

CALLIE PACED the interview room at the county jail after having made record time on a return trip through the mountains. At the last minute, she'd veered from her intended path of interrogating David's mother because doing so felt like a form of torture when the woman was obviously fragile and lost.

Callie would use the note first in an attempt to shake David out of his intransigence. She might have to resort to using his mother as a threat, but she hoped not. To that end, she'd decided an emotional appeal would have to work, and their only connection— besides one night that he had already destroyed—was their shared past.

She didn't have a lot of optimism that the sketchy note would sway him, but she also knew better than to put any concrete information in writing. Prisoners had rights, yes, but that didn't extend to blind acceptance of sealed envelopes or containers by the authorities. She'd thought about various codes she might use, but she and David had been apart too long for that to work.

Please, David. She paced again to the far corner of the concrete block room. *Please talk to me.*

When she heard the door opening, she was almost afraid to turn.

But then she heard the sound of heavy, shortened steps, like those of a prisoner whose ankles were bound. She bit her lower lip and revolved to face him.

The man who had thrilled her, had sent her to stunning heights…that man was nowhere in evidence. Neither was the one who had given himself up to her embrace.

Before her stood a stranger, not the one who'd raged at her, not the one who'd smoldered with anger. This man was solid stone, refusing to so much as meet her eyes.

"Please remove his cuffs," she requested of the deputy.

A quick, impatient shake of David's head. "No. This won't take long."

The deputy looked between them as if trying to figure out whom to obey.

David's eyes remained locked on the wall above her head, but she could see his jaw flexing.

To avoid causing him further grief, she merely nodded at the deputy, who shook his head and left the room.

David said nothing, did nothing.

For one of the few times in her life, Callie didn't know what to say. At last she ventured a question. "Wouldn't you be more comfortable if they uncuffed you?"

"This is reality. It's who I am."

But it's not, she wanted to protest. A night without sleep, a day of upheaval…suddenly, Callie was exhausted, sick of everything. "What are you trying to accomplish by acting like this?"

At last his gaze flicked to hers. "Just go away, Callie."

If his voice hadn't been surprisingly gentle, perhaps she would have thrown up her hands. "I can't."

His jaw clenched. "Why the hell not?"

"What do you want from me, David? Your attorney's out of town, and I'm trying to help you. You don't have to be alone in this, but you slap away every attempt—" Seeing his hardened features, frustration rose.

"All right!" she exploded. "No more kid gloves." She slapped her palms on the table. "Tell me about Ned Compton."

At last she'd succeeded in shaking him. "What?"

"I want to know about your life with your stepfather."

His whole face tightened. "Don't call him that."

An inkling grew into a much stronger instinct. Ned Compton. Why hadn't she seen it before? Callie had had to learn to trust her intuition; sometimes it made all the difference in a case. She'd been sleepwalking since she'd lost her confidence in her skills. Now the driven prosecutor was back and on the hunt. "What did he do to you, David? Did he hit you? What was he like when nobody was looking?"

She saw the reaction, so faint she would have missed it if she hadn't been staring straight at him.

"He was fine." Back to not meeting her gaze.

"You don't kill someone who's… '*fine.*'" She punctuated the word with fingers clenched in quotation marks. "What are you hiding?"

He ignored the question. "You have no idea what I was like back then."

"Only months after you played Sir Galahad with

me? I don't buy that, David. You reached out to a messed-up girl who was a total stranger, and you stuck with me even when it cost you dearly." She started around the table. "How you treated me was no different than you treated everyone else. Everybody loved you. You changed that much after I left? Uh-uh." She folded her arms in front of her chest. "I think I might need to have a chat with your mother."

His eyes flew wide, then narrowed to pure fury. Rage pumped off him in rolling waves.

Abruptly, he simply shrugged. Turned off his feelings like a spigot. "She wasn't there that night. She can't tell you anything."

"She just walked in on you after you'd killed him, is that right?" That's what his testimony had been.

"Yeah." His gaze locked on hers as if daring her to argue. "My fingerprints were on the murder weapon. Do your homework."

She let the insult pass. "So the person who sent me an anonymous note that Ned Compton is the key was…?" She left the question hanging, alert for the slightest reaction.

The smallest things could betray a person—the faint widening of the eye, the tiniest hitch of breath, the quick flinch of a muscle.

She spotted all three. David was not the accomplished liar she'd learned to be.

"Someone's just messing with your head," he said. "You don't have time to hang around anyway. Your job is on the line, you told me so."

It was her turn to react as he stated what she'd been trying to ignore. She did not have the luxury of lingering here, had indeed planned to leave today and return to fight for her career, her life, the only one she knew.

She could relinquish Miss Margaret's legacy and figure out some way not to harm the people involved. She had two weeks left on her thirty days, but that wasn't an insurmountable issue, she had to believe.

But if she went back now, David would stay in jail until his trial, then he would go back to Jackson, to a cell that would cage his spirit, that would harden him beyond redemption, the traces that were left of that beautiful boy. This time prison might even break him.

"You're absolutely right. It makes no sense for me to remain here," she said, testing him.

"Good." Relief warred with the faintest spark of grief, then both settled into resignation bordering on despair.

So what did she say to him when she knew she had no intention of leaving? When she planned to drive straight to his mother's house and force the truth she was beginning to suspect? Did she walk away and let desolation settle deep into his bones for however long was required for her to dig out what had really happened that night?

But what if she were wrong? Did she dare raise his hopes?

Someone knew the truth of Ned Compton's death. She'd hoped to shake it from David, but he hadn't blinked. Locked up, he couldn't interfere with her, and maybe that was what she needed, even though seeing him chained grieved her.

She felt him staring at her and looked up, realizing she'd been silent too long. "So…can I bring you anything?" she said with careful politeness.

"No." His brow beetled. "Thanks," he added as an afterthought, his gaze piercing. *What are you up to?* she could almost hear him asking.

She watched his fingers—those long, powerful fingers that had caressed her body, had drawn her soul from her—clench, and she had a moment's temptation to yell at him, to shout, *What are you doing to yourself? To us? To what we could be together?*

But even if she succeeded in getting to the bottom of this tangle and freeing him, she didn't know what his dreams were, what he'd wish to salvage from the bright future that had been torn from him…and she had her own goals, her own game plan.

One thing at a time, she lectured herself.

"Okay, then. I'll see you later." She eased toward the door.

"Callie." His voice was ominous. "Where are you going?"

She skirted around him.

"Don't involve my mother in this, you hear me?"

The urgency in his tone was wrenching. She was on the right track, had to be. She slipped through the cell opening, biting her lip as she heard the jerky half steps caused by his ankle bindings.

"Callie!" His tormented roar echoed in her head.

I'm doing this for you, David. She was practically running as she left.

"Mrs. Langley? It's Callie Hunter," she called as she knocked for the second time. "I need to speak with you about David."

The drapes were closed, the door was locked. Callie decided, after a third round of knocking, to circle the house and see if she could detect anyone inside.

Once more, the woman's sad plight touched her. The small home that had always been neat and well tended had fallen into decay. David's efforts were slowly reversing the trend, but the sense of hopelessness was inescapable. For a second, Callie contemplated simply retracing her steps and letting the woman be.

But that would not save David.

When Callie had first learned of his criminal record, she had assumed that everything bad that had happened had begun with her, that his fall from favor was solely her fault.

Only today had she stopped to consider that Ned Compton had entered David's life at that same juncture. She'd never met the man, though she had heard his name mentioned when she lived here. He'd been new in town then, she thought, and wealthy compared to the rest of Oak Hollow.

Not that she expected to escape blame herself. She had surely initiated David's precipitous decline, and she bore plenty of responsibility for taking a decent boy and so ruthlessly pursuing him that the normal drives of a teenage male had led him straight into her very willing arms.

He would never have touched her if he'd known she

was only fourteen. She'd understood that then and even more so now.

Still, Delia Langley had never given any indication of wanting a husband. She'd been an exceedingly beautiful woman, but her life had been centered around David, and even a dumb teenage girl could see all that she'd sacrificed to raise a very fine boy.

So how had Ned Compton come into the picture? And what kind of man had he been really?

A tiny stir in the curtains of the back bedroom caught Callie's eye.

Gotcha.

She strode up the back steps and tried the screen door. Finding it locked, she rapped sharply on its frame. "Mrs. Langley, when I left David at the jail, he was chained hand and foot. He'll go back to prison for a long time if something doesn't change."

Was that faint sound footsteps? Just in case, she continued. "I think there's more to the story than anyone knows. I also think you're the one who sent me that note—"

The back door opened. "Chained?" His mother's hand went to her throat.

"Yes. Did you send me that note?"

Unpainted lips pressed together. She nodded.

"He doesn't want me talking to you," Callie said. "But if I don't, there's no help for him."

"Please." The screen door opened. "Come inside."

Callie followed her.

"Would you like some tea?" His mother's hands fluttered like wounded birds.

Callie trod carefully, though she wanted to scream, *Talk to me now!* Witnesses could be spooked so easily, and this woman was teetering on the sharp edge of falling apart. "Yes, thank you."

With jerky steps, Mrs. Langley moved to the cabinet and drew out a glass, then opened the freezer compartment of the ancient refrigerator and took out ice cubes. She dipped into the refrigerator section and withdrew a plastic pitcher.

The pitcher suddenly tumbled to the floor, splattering tea everywhere.

With the hoarse cry of someone stretched beyond her limits, Delia Langley fell to her knees, oblivious to the pool of brown liquid around her.

"It was me," she choked out. "He was trying to protect me, and I was—I couldn't—" She extended her arms, beseeching Callie, for what she couldn't say. Mercy? Forgiveness?

What exactly had David done? Nauseated by what she was beginning to suspect, Callie went to the woman ineffectively attempting to mop up the liquid with a dish towel and pulled her to her feet.

"I—I need to—" Mrs. Langley gestured to the floor. "I have to—" Normally a graceful, contained woman, she was shaking and spreading the mess to her clothing.

"Come here." Callie used the most soothing tone she could manage, given her own agitation. "I'll take care of it."

But Delia continued to mop and was only making things worse. Callie cast around until she found a drawer with more towels and went to work on the mess, hoping David's mother would calm down as the puddle receded.

At last they were done. Callie deposited the stained towels in the washing machine and turned to the woman standing in the middle of the kitchen as if in a trance.

Pity swamped Callie. Whatever exactly David had done, she thought she understood why. The woman before her was a frail wisp. She'd had the strength to raise David, to care for him alone and struggle every day to feed him and put a roof over his head until he was big enough to help.

The price of that, though, had to be steep. Had the incessant battle to keep them afloat stolen all her strength?

Or had the events of that tragic night finally broken her? Callie wasn't sure, but it was time to find out.

"Let's sit." She led Delia to the table and seated her in a chair, then pulled another one near. "I need you to tell me exactly what happened, for David's sake."

The vacant stare turned to her. A tiny flicker told Callie she was still in there, the woman who had raised him, had loved him. "He made me promise. After. I didn't—I couldn't— By the time I recovered myself, began to understand what he'd done, it was too late. He'd already…" Her shoulders rounded, her voice became a whisper. "Still, I should have done some-thing…." Her entire body began to quake. "I will never forgive myself. I'm his mother. I should have…"

Callie had to get the story from her before she fell

apart completely. She clasped Delia's hands and squeezed. "You know David loves you," she began.

If anything, Delia curled in on herself even more.

"Mrs. Langley, if you care about your son, you have to get a grip on yourself and talk to me. We're running out of time. He's in a dangerous situation. He could be sent back to prison very soon."

"No—" she cried, her head lifting, her eyes sparking. "He can't! He did nothing. It was me, I told you!"

And then Callie began to truly understand.

She'd had it all wrong. "David didn't kill Ned Compton, not even in defense of you, did he? It was you, and David took the fall."

"Yes!" His mother covered her face with her hands and broke into racking sobs.

Oh my God. Fifteen years of hell. Endless hate aimed in his direction.

A life fractured. Dreams ground to dust.

And none of it his fault. The David she'd loved—still loved, she might as well accept—had, in one selfless act, sacrificed everything he'd ever hoped for to protect the woman who'd given him life. He would have seen it as proper and just, that noble boy upon whose shoulders so much had been heaped.

Where is the justice? Callie wanted to cry.

She believed in the system—it was necessary to survive every day in the grim world that she inhabited. But sometimes there were cases that literally made you sick, that robbed you of even the slimmest threads of faith in a just world. Of the conviction that good could triumph.

Oh, David. She wanted to weep for him, but that would do no good. It was time to fight for him.

With every weapon in her armory.

"Mrs. Langley." She recognized the signs now and wondered why no one else had. "How long had Ned Compton abused you?"

The older woman shuddered, but she only kept sobbing, more softly now.

Callie longed to ask Delia how she could keep silent for so long, but Callie had seen too many victims of abuse not to realize that while many of them could be saved, some were broken in a way that was beyond mending.

She harnessed the urge to berate this pitiful creature and instead took Delia Langley in her arms, holding her as she wept.

Inside Callie, though, drumbeats sounded. The clock ticked away the minutes of imprisonment David should not be enduring. "Mrs. Langley, it's not too late. You can help David now. Your son needs you, but he will never ask." She felt the slight body tense. "Will you let him go back to prison?"

Delia Langley's head rose swiftly, her reddened eyes fierce. "No. I could not—" She trembled, then forced herself to straighten. "I could not bear it." She pressed her lips together to still them. "But I don't know what to do."

"That's okay," Callie said. "I do."

"You must hate me," his mother said. "He must, though he's never even hinted at it, not once." She glanced away, eyes batting hard. "How could I have been so weak? My boy, my precious boy—" She covered her mouth with one hand and began to crumple again.

"Stop it." Callie knew she sounded cruel, but time was racing past. "Mrs. Langley, if you want to help David, you have to keep it together." Then she relented. "I don't hate you. He doesn't, either. He loves you."

"Delia," she said, straightening. "Why don't you call me Delia." She drew in a deep breath. "Every day—" She locked her gaze on Callie's. "Every day since they took him away, I have loathed myself for bringing that man into our lives. He was handsome and charming and so strong. I thought I was doing the right thing, giving David a father figure, someone who was admired by the community, someone who could help him back on the path after he lost his way with—" She faltered.

"With me." Callie nodded. "You can say that. I've earned it. If he had never met me…" She shook her head. "I bear my own share of guilt in this, Mrs.— Delia. I started him down this path."

"You were so young. And that poor baby…"

Callie clenched her fingers into fists against that trip down memory lane. "We can't focus on that right now. We have to save David. There are those who are eager to send him back to prison, and we have to stop them."

"Tell me what to do."

Callie tried to think of an answer. She didn't want David being held one second longer than necessary, but her hands were tied until his attorney returned.

Albert Manning. He wasn't a criminal attorney, but he was licensed in Georgia. She could guide his steps.

But she couldn't get ahead of herself. She had to know precisely what they were dealing with. "I need the whole story. Explain to me exactly what happened."

Delia's lips quivered, but she quickly settled herself. Then she sat ramrod straight and began to talk.

"I don't know why Ned Compton took an interest in me. I'm no one special."

Callie could have argued with her; Delia Langley was—or had been—a very striking woman, just like her handsome son. Callie had often admired her, back before the ravages of time and grief had washed out her beauty. Now she was painfully thin and didn't look well at all.

"Later, when I could think about it, I suppose there were two parts to what brought him here. David seemed to gather all the light into him, and everyone wanted to be near him, to bask in the glow he cast off." She glanced at Callie. "You know how he was, everyone's hero." At Callie's nod, she continued. "I suppose that was part of it—Ned had a hunger to be the center of everything. When David met you and…" She looked down.

Callie didn't need her to fill in the words. "When I tarnished his image, you mean."

Delia pressed her lips together. "Once you were gone, David had a difficult time getting over all the emotional upheaval. He started missing class, and his athletic performance suffered. Ned saw his opening. He could put the town's star back on the straight and narrow and be a hero for it. He began to come around, and he was always kind and supportive. I was at my wits' end. Never before had David been rebellious with me, and I could see his future going down the drain." She rubbed her brow. "So when Ned suggested we marry and make him David's stepfather, I thought…" For long seconds, she stared off into obviously painful memories.

"I was so tired, you see, and everything I'd tried to do seemed hopeless. I began to rely too much on Ned, and he took over more and more. I still don't—" Her voice caught.

She gathered herself together, gripping her arms tightly. "Things changed when Ned moved us into his house. I'd never lived in a fine place like that, so at first I was uneasy, and when he would correct me, I'd just think of how uneducated I was and I'd try harder, but nothing was ever enough and he—" She paused to compose herself, but all the color had drained from her face. She looked ancient.

"The first time he hit me, I was so shocked I didn't— I couldn't figure out what to do. David's father would never have…" She pressed trembling lips together before going on with her story.

She didn't really need to. Callie had heard this tale hundreds of times. "Was David aware of it then?" He surely had been later.

"No." A violent shake of her head. "It was—Ned was already so hard on him, and things kept getting worse between them. I couldn't let David know or he might…" Delia's gaze beseeched her. "It was an accident, I swear it. David was only trying to stop him from beating me. He'd suspected, I realize now, and tried to make me confirm it, but Ned was very clever.

When David confronted him and accused him, Ned threatened him. Said no one would ever believe him now, not after he'd thrown away his future the way he had. That he had the town in his pocket. That—" Her voice broke. "That David couldn't watch me all the time." Tears spilled over. "David begged me to leave him. Said he could get a job and support us, that all I had to do was leave with him and he'd take care of me."

She closed her eyes. "If only I'd gone, but I was frightened of Ned, and David was struggling. He needed to finish school, to get back on track. *'Go off to college and make a life,'* I said, but he told me he couldn't leave me. And then, one night, Ned struck me in front of him. David went crazy, jumped on him...the fight was terrible. David was young and strong, but Ned had no sense of honor. He went for David's knees, said he'd cripple my boy so he wouldn't be able to play football and he'd be stuck here forever, never amounting to anything. He said cruel, awful things about me, and David's rage made him reckless where Ned was so canny. He caught David off guard and toppled him to the floor on his back. He was about to smash his foot into David's knee—"

She looked so gray that Callie reached out for her. "Delia, you don't have to continue."

But it was as if Delia were locked in that time and couldn't hear her. "He said he'd call his buddy the sheriff and have David charged with assault. Said David would go to jail and lose everything. Ned was kicking him, hurting him...I couldn't let him destroy my son. I grabbed the first thing I could find to stop him—the fire-place poker." She turned horrified eyes to Callie. "I didn't mean to kill him. I only wanted to stop him, but I hit him once and then he wheeled on me, and I swung again and it— His head…there was blood, so much blood. I dropped the poker. I must have fainted because the next thing I knew, the sheriff was there, putting David in handcuffs and—" She began to gasp for air.

Then, like a rag doll, she simply collapsed to the floor.

"Delia!" Callie rushed to her, feeling frantically for a pulse. She had little knowledge of first aid, but Delia's heart rate was clearly unsteady. Callie raced for the phone and dialed for help, afraid it would take too long in this remote spot. When the dispatcher assured her help would be there in fifteen or twenty minutes and patched her in to the paramedics so they could advise her what to do in the meantime, Callie was too busy to think beyond keeping Delia alive.

Hours later, Delia had been admitted overnight to the county hospital for observation after what the doctors believed was a panic attack exacerbated by Delia's poor physical condition. Exhausted, Callie was desperate for sleep, but she couldn't rest yet.

David was in jail, and she had to set in motion the process to clear him.

But first, before he heard about his mother from someone else, she had to go see him.

And confess what she'd done.

CHAPTER SEVENTEEN

SHE APPROACHED the interview room like a condemned prisoner on the way to the gallows. She'd been wise enough not to demand anything from the sheriff regarding David's release; one charge would not suddenly vanish simply because another had been invalidated. She would have to talk to the D.A., and she'd have to choose every step from here carefully.

Right now, tonight, she was only here on an errand of mercy. The sheriff had no idea how she longed to be anywhere else.

David would hate her. As well he should.

It was with relief that she noted that he was only handcuffed this time, not ankle-bound, as well. Even a reviled criminal like David deserved, apparently, a little consideration when bad news was coming his way.

He stood, as before, braced against whatever she had to say. The sight of those broad shoulders stiffened to deflect whatever toll she would exact made her inexpressibly sad.

She was the enemy. *And I am.* She accepted the role, however unwelcome. Most of the troubles in David's life had begun with her.

She thought of a tiny grave, a precious memorial, and she wondered if she would ever finish paying for all the damage she'd created. With a deep inhalation, she steeled herself and opened the door.

He turned, his face a mask, a stone wall. Obviously expecting the worst.

She decided to rip off the bandage, quick and clean, since there was no easy way to say what she had to tell him. "Your mother is in the hospital. She's going to be all right, though. She just needs rest and nourishment," she hurried to reassure.

None of that helped one iota, she could tell.

His glare was acid. Fire and brimstone. "What have you done?"

Callie averted her gaze. There was no excusing her, no rationalization that the hardened man would accept. "I'm sorry."

"Sorry?" He advanced on her, then abruptly stopped as the deputy rattled the knob from outside.

David didn't come closer but his face lost all pretense of control. *"Sorry?"* he echoed. A muscle hardened in his jaw. "Tell me." Not a request.

"She's the one who sent me the note. She's desperate to help you," Callie tried.

"She promised she'd never—"

"David, you're innocent. You should never have—" Seeing his face go from fury to outright loathing, she halted. Continuing took everything she had. "All of this can go away," she whispered furiously. "If everyone knew what really happened, no one—"

"Stop it." He bit off each word. "Do not say it. Don't you dare." Then utter devastation ravaged his features. "You have made a travesty of the last fifteen years of my life." He hadn't approached, yet he seemed to loom. "Is that what you want? For me to have wasted everything, all my dreams, every single thing I ever hoped for?" His voice caught, and he had to look away.

As he struggled to compose himself, Callie tried to think how to frame her argument. "David, I can—"

Viciously he cut her off. "You can't do anything. Not one goddamn thing, do you hear me?" His nostrils flared and his eyes burned. "Haven't you done enough damage?" He glared at her like some creature he loathed. "If I'd never met you…"

Her eyes burned. She forced herself to battle back the agony that threatened to destroy her. Of course he was right. Meeting her had begun his descent into endless loss. He'd pitied her. His kind, generous heart had taken up for her when she'd had no one else. He'd always been the champion of the downtrodden, and he'd done for his mother what he'd done for her…put them before what he really wanted. Given up all to help someone else.

"I can save her," she beseeched. "I can save you, too."

He turned on her, quick and savage. "Do you think I want anything from you? After what you've done? Do you not get it that she would never survive a trial? Even if you could clear her—" his withering tone spoke of his utter lack of confidence "—doesn't today demonstrate that she can't survive the process of your precious justice system?" It was clear that he couldn't stand the sight of her.

The dingy gray walls matched her spirits, but somehow Callie had to think her way past her devastation. She could free him now, she knew it. Could clear his mother. "Listen to me. There's is a defense that—"

"Get out!" he roared. "Get out of my life!"

The deputy shoved the door open. Callie rushed to reassure him. "It's all right, Deputy. I'm fine."

The man pinned David with a warning gaze. "I better not see you one foot closer to her than you are now. As a matter of fact, you back away."

"No problem." David's loathing gaze caught her. "I have nothing else to say to Ms. Hunter."

She'd heard her name spoken in many contexts, but never with such animosity.

She somehow found her voice when what she really wanted to do was break down. "Thank you, Deputy."

Silence reigned while they waited for the man to close the door again.

When it came, David's voice was cold as the grave. "For the sake of that child," he said, invoking her plea to him. "Go away now. And don't ever come back."

That child. Not our baby.

He'd written her out of his life for good.

"David, please…you have to let me fix this." If she had to plead, so be it. She couldn't bear to leave things this way.

He stared at the opposite wall. "You can't."

Everything in Callie cried out to stay, to make him see, to reassure him that she could…

Her shoulders sank in defeat. Everything she touched eventually turned to ashes. He was right, much as it sickened her to admit it. The most she could do for him now was to turn over what she'd learned to his attorney.

"I'm so sorry," she whispered brokenly. Then she summoned what strength was left to her and did as he asked.

Began making plans to pack up and drive out of his life.

SHE'D GOTTEN TEN MILES down the road back to Oak Hollow when she realized that she had two allegiances—one to David, who loathed the sight of her and wanted her gone. He'd made that perfectly, brutally clear.

But she'd also made a promise to his mother. Before she ran out of town with her tail tucked between her legs—oh, how that prospect grated on her, however much she'd wronged him—she couldn't just disappear without talking to Delia, as least putting her mind at ease that she had a viable defense, that what David feared was not the case.

She turned the car around and drove toward the hospital.

Callie was certain of little right now, but one thing she believed to her marrow was that Delia Langley could be defended. She should not have to worry about her fate. Any competent attorney could ensure that she would spend not one hour in jail.

Except Delia couldn't afford that competent attorney.

In that instant, Callie saw what she could do to redeem herself. Miss Margaret had left Callie with the resources to buy the best defense Delia Langley could ever wish for.

And maybe, just maybe, that attorney could swing

the tide for David, as well. Surely if even Mickey Patton understood the sacrifice David had made, he or one of his buddies would recant the assault charge. Of course she would have to dig up evidence that Ned Compton had a history of abuse, but if there were previous girl-friends or—

There she went again, getting involved. *Haven't you done enough damage?*

But how could he expect her just to walk away? She banged her fist on the steering wheel. He was wrong, damn him. She could fix this, all of it, if only…

The image of his face, ravaged, despairing, would not let her be. She sagged against the seat, watching an inner slide show of this thoroughly decent man and the noble boy he'd once been. Could she be absolutely posi-tive that she could clear him of the current charges?

No. She of all people knew the justice system was ca-pricious. Wasn't that why she hadn't revealed that her witness had an ulterior motive regarding the defendant? Because she didn't fully trust that a bad guy would pay?

She raked her fingers through her hair.

In the end the bad guy hadn't paid anyway.

If she were really honest with herself, she knew that the frightening reality was that David could lose. That she no longer trusted herself to save him.

This was why she'd chosen prosecution and not defense. Why she'd done everything possible to keep her heart out of the courtroom. Prosecutors focused on wrong and right, on the black and white of guilt or in-nocence. She'd liked the moral high ground of it.

At least she had as long as her feet had been planted safely there. She knew how to excel after a childhood full of failure, and she'd liked the air up there on the peaks. Success didn't endanger her heart, and a sure knowledge of her position as a fighter for good over evil had been the armor that had shielded her.

Until she'd faltered, that is. Felt the sweat of fear as her first defeat, the first chink in the casing she'd donned to clearly delineate the woman from the mixed-up girl, had begun to eat away at her faith in herself.

Now she was mired in uncertainty, too much of the insecure girl bubbling up to the surface and blistering the patina of the woman she'd believed herself to be.

She was terrified of falling, sliding down that peak. She'd been kidding herself and playing house these past few days with David. Pretending that there could be more for her than the job that was the sum total of her, the burning ambition that provided the only warmth in a life constructed on cold calculation.

Her job might have lost its shine even before she'd faltered.

But it was all she had.

Callie stepped from her car in the hospital parking lot and felt for the first time since she'd arrived back in Georgia a return of her strength. She had been Lady Justice before; she could be again. All she had to do was lock up the past and throw away the key. Never let herself be touched by it again.

Just as she would never be touched by David again, physically or emotionally.

If her heart quailed a bit at the notion, she ruthlessly stamped out any weakness. She couldn't afford it. She would never survive if she let herself think about what she'd lost here, in this place that seemed destined to forever haunt her.

Outside the three-story redbrick building, Callie drew in a deep, steadying breath.

Then marched inside to tie up one last loose end before she would leave Oak Hollow forever.

SHE SHUDDERED a little as she made her way down the beige hallway, the sting of disinfectants the strongest note in the powerful bouquet that was a hospital. She thought back to the pale, fragile figure she'd comforted while waiting for the ambulance, every second a tick of fear that she'd wind up telling David she'd killed his mother.

Though how that could have provoked a much worse reaction from him remained to be seen.

Not fair, Callie. He's given up everything for her.

She couldn't think about David anymore, how badly she'd blundered with him. Instead she braced herself for the wraith she would find as she pushed open the door to Delia's room.

But if she'd expected a fragile, clinging victim, she was dead wrong.

"Is David out of jail?" demanded Delia. She was still pale, still hooked up to an IV, but the moment Callie entered, she used the controls to raise the head of her bed, never taking her eyes off Callie. "Where is he?"

"He's—it's— He's still there, Delia."

"Why? I told you I did it. Why haven't they let him go?"

"It's not that simple. He's already served his time for Ned Compton's death. He's in jail because of the assault charges. He'll have to have a hearing on the most recent one."

"Why haven't you gotten him out on bail, at the very least? He shouldn't be in there. You know what being locked up is doing to him. Do I need to pledge my house? Will that help? Go back and tell them I'll give up whatever I have. He's not the guilty one, I am."

The intricacies of the legal system were clearly lost on his mother, and that wasn't the point of this visit anyway. "I'll make his attorney aware of everything I know. He'll be back in two days."

"Two days? My son can't stay there that long. You do it. You know how."

Callie's shoulders sank. "He's refused my help. He—" *Hates me,* she almost said, but that was between them. "I'm leaving town. He's been very clear that he wants nothing else to do with me, and frankly I can't blame him." She looked straight at Delia. "I've fought him at every turn, I haven't listened to anything he's asked. I owe him more than that after all the harm I've done."

Delia's gaze bored into her. "So you're just going to give up?" She leaned forward, her face pale but her eyes burning coals as she gripped Callie's hand. "You could actually walk away and leave him in jail? What kind of person are you?"

I don't know, she wanted to cry out. Had she ever

known who she was, except a child who wasn't wanted, a girl who caused trouble…a woman who kept herself apart from everyone who might matter? She tore herself from Delia's grasp and began to pace. "Delia, he can't stand the sight of me. He's— Look what he did to save you, and now he's furious and worried sick that you'll go to jail, too, that I'll destroy you where Ned Compton couldn't."

At Delia's gasp, Callie turned, hurried over. "You won't, Delia, I swear it. I'm going to hire you the best lawyer in the state of Georgia, and you'll be fine, I promise."

"I want you."

"What?" Callie shook her head. "No, you don't understand. I've told you I can't— Delia, I'm not a defense attorney. Even if I were, I can't practice here, I explained that."

"You said you could work with someone who is." Green eyes so much like David's looked up at her from a face shadowed with exhaustion yet burning with an inner resolve. "I can get a loan on my house and hire you if that's what it takes."

"No! No, of course you can't do that. I don't want your money, it's not that, it's—"

"Don't you love my son?"

The question was so simple it stole her breath. She should have had to think about the answer.

But even after all the antagonism, she didn't. "Yes," she said softly, then louder. "Yes, I love him, but—"

"Then who could defend us better?"

There was one possibility called *pro hac vice* in which Callie could petition the court for permission to practice for one particular case in a single court, but there was the rub—one case, not two. Delia and David should have different counsel anyway to protect each of them to the maximum. She could try one case and assist on the other, but defense wasn't her expertise and how she could she gamble with either of their lives?

"He won't want me," she pointed out.

"Leave that to me. You just go to work getting him out of jail and finding someone who's licensed in Georgia. Couldn't Albert Manning do it, if you're calling the shots?"

Callie looked at Delia with new respect. *Great minds think alike.* "He could. If he will, that is."

"Don't lawyers argue for a living?"

Callie stared at the woman emerging before her. This was the Delia who'd spent her life fighting to make a future for her son, the one who'd created the golden boy.

But then she remembered the shuttered man, the one who wanted her out of his life.

Haven't you done enough damage?

"I can't, Delia."

"What? Are you serious?"

"I don't mean I won't help, but I—I have to leave. My job—I could lose it. I can't stay here any longer." At Delia's protest, she raised a hand. "I'll talk to Albert before I go, tell him what to do right now. He'll have suggestions for the best person to represent David. I'm also hiring a lawyer for you, though I don't think a good prosecutor will want to take you to trial. But—" she locked eyes on Delia "—David's right. I've barged in, with the best of intentions maybe, but he craves control over his life after all the years he's had none, and I've undercut him, thinking I knew better."

Stony silence, but no argument. Callie continued. "He deserves at least that respect. However wrong-headed I think he's been, I understand it, don't you? He's a noble man with more inner strength than anyone I've ever met, even you. Which is really saying something."

Delia's mouth curved slightly but her eyes were worried.

"I've hurt him too much, Delia, first when I derailed his plans back then because I craved what I sensed in him—his strength and his goodness. I've been doing it again because I needed to prove myself. Wanted to be the one rescuing him this time." Callie had to look away, blinking rapidly. "However angry he is about it, his secret is out, and it's the key to saving him. I'd give a lot to be the one doing it, but love, what little I understand of it, means not barreling over the person you care for."

"Callie, how could anyone defend him better than you?"

Callie started to speak but couldn't. After a moment she gathered her composure. "I'll monitor each step, I promise. I'll spend every last penny of Miss Margaret's estate to make sure he's a free man and that you're taken care of, too. I wish—" She struggled past the lump in her throat. "I wish it could be me—God knows I owe him—but that debt is exactly why I have to walk away as he wants me to. Everything I know about goodness begins with that boy who stood beside me, and to hurt him any more than I already have…"

She couldn't stay any longer. "I'll set everything in motion immediately, and if you need me, here's my card. I'll put my cell number on the back. If you have the slightest worry, you don't hesitate to call me," she said fiercely. "I won't let you down, I swear it. Whatever it takes. And I won't let him down, either."

Before she fell apart completely, Callie thrust her card into the woman's hands and raced out the door.

CHAPTER EIGHTEEN

IT HAD BEEN the longest night of his life.

He'd had some bad ones before—that first night in a cell as a scared kid, shaking inside so badly he was afraid he'd break down and embarrass himself.

Or the one right before he'd known he would be locked up for fifteen years…no high school prom, no graduation, no college, no football.

No future.

That first night at Jackson, the one that could still make him shudder in sympathy for that poor mixed-up kid who'd held on to the image of his mother safe in her bed. That image was all that had gotten him through the nightmare of the tattooed hulk in the bunk beneath him, the sounds all around that he couldn't begin to block out.

Enough. He would rejoin that world soon enough. Callie could say all she wanted to about saving him, but he was past redemption now. There was a fire deep in his gut that would never go out, a burning anger that nothing on this earth seemed able to smother.

He stared at the dark, cracked ceiling and wondered how his life got so screwed up.

I can save her. I can save you, too.

Oh, Callie… For a moment he stopped resenting her, the criminal waste of what she'd done. Thought about that one night they'd spent together until he couldn't stand it anymore.

All that was over with and done. There would be no rescue for him.

Happy endings were for other people.

Now he just had to figure out how to limit the damage to his mother. He should have made Callie swear she would never tell a soul about what she'd heard.

He could take being locked up. His mother couldn't.

And damned if he'd allow his salvation to be the instrument of her destruction.

He thrust himself from the cot and began to pace. When was his sorry attorney coming back? His fingers molded into a fist as he eyed the wall and wished he could just flail away at it, pound out the rage that simmered within him as he recalled the hurt on Callie's face, thought about his mother lying in a hospital somewhere—hell, he didn't even know where she was and she might die from all the strain, frail as she was.

His shoulders hunched and he raked his fingers through his hair.

"Langley. You got visitors."

He wheeled. "What?"

"Yeah. Come on."

David had lost all sense of time, but it couldn't be much past dawn. "Who is it?"

"Your attorney. You comin' or not?"

He exhaled in a gust, worn from the sleepless hours. "Yeah." He steeled himself to argue his mother's case, should Callie have interfered already.

Please let me fix this.

Brown eyes, deep wells of pain.

Leave me alone, Callie.

Ruthlessly he extinguished all thoughts of her and walked toward the cell door, already extending his wrists for the bonds that he'd better get used to.

Christ, he was so tired.

A few moments later, the deputy led him into the same interview room that was inextricably tied with Callie for him. He glanced around, almost hoping…

Of course not. To his regret, at last she'd listened.

Then the door opened again, and resignation was replaced with shock. "Mom?"

"Oh, sweetheart." His mother crossed to him.

"What are you doing here?" He held her at arm's length. "You should be in the hospital."

A second figure entered the room.

"Mr. Manning."

"Hello, David." The older man, usually stiff with disapproval of him, seemed mired in regret. "Your mother and I need to talk to you."

David glanced back and forth between them. He leaned near his mother and whispered. "You haven't told anyone, have you? Please, Mom—"

She gripped his hands, and he could see the sorrow as she took in the sight of the cuffs. "Everything's going to be all right, sweetheart. Come sit."

He remained standing. "Where's my attorney? What are you doing here?"

Manning sighed. "First of all, my deepest apologies. We all have done you a grievous wrong. As for Ned…"

David's head whipped around. "You *told* him?" he accused his mother.

"David, I couldn't let you suffer anymore."

"Mom, no!" The cry was dragged from the depths of his soul. He glared at the attorney. "She's lying. Don't believe a word she says."

The older man eyed him with sympathy and what might be fondness. "Callie said you would try to deny it, but it's too late, son."

David closed his eyes. Felt the avalanche crashing down upon him. Suddenly so weary he couldn't stand, he sank into the nearest chair and let his head fall into his hands. Where did he go from here, when all he'd given up was now rendered meaningless? "Damn you, Callie," he murmured.

"Don't you dare, David William Langley. Don't you curse that girl. Do you not understand that everything she's done is because she loves you? She's fighting for you—are you just going to give up?"

Why shouldn't he? "It's no use, Mom. I'm an ex-con, about to go to jail for the second time. I'll forever be marked. There's nowhere up from here, don't you get it?" He sat up straight and leaned closer. "Please don't tell anyone. What happened stays inside this room. I can take it—I've learned how to survive in there. You couldn't. It would kill you. You have to leave this alone."

"Callie says she can get me off." His mother's expression showed the first strains of doubt.

"Callie's gone. We're on our own, the way we always have been. You have to leave this in my hands. I can't take chances with you. Look at what happened already—you wound up in the hospital. Do you honestly think you can take the pressure of a trial?"

She gripped his hand. "My poor boy. How much you have suffered, all because I was weak."

"It's okay, I can handle it. Please." He included both of them in his request. "Just let this go."

"No, not anymore. Sweetheart, don't you see what you're doing to yourself? You've lost so much of your life, but you don't have to sacrifice any more." She squeezed his fingers. "I know trust comes hard now. Anyone would feel that way in your place, but David, your heart has been scarred enough. There's a woman out there who desperately wants to help you, if only you'd let her. Can't you, just once, lean on someone else?"

He looked at her, stunned. He thought about the pain on Callie's face, the slump of her shoulders as she'd left, believing he hated her. However hard he'd tried, the bleak hours of soul-searching last night had taught him that one thing he could not do was hate Callie Hunter.

Could he actually take that leap of faith?

And was it fair to her if he did?

"She's been hurt, too, Mom. And she has a life elsewhere."

His mother drew a card from her purse. "Albert, do you by chance have a cell phone?"

The older man nodded. "Despise the damn thing, but my son insisted." He drew it out of his pocket and extended it to David.

"On the back of this card is Callie's cell phone number. Will you give the future a chance?"

Two faces watched him, willing him to accept. Wasn't calling her only setting them both up for more misery?

When did you become such a coward? The thought stopped him in his tracks.

He dropped his head. Stared at the metal binding his hands.

He'd long ago lost faith in a world that was fair. Had closed himself off from everyone and everything because the price of caring was too steep, wielded a killing blow.

But within him was one tiny seed of the boy he'd been, the one who'd had limitless faith in himself and his ability to conquer anything.

This point, he sensed, was where that seed had a chance to grow…or died forever.

If he could take a leap of faith that seemed taller than the highest mountain.

He thought about the one night he and Callie had loved with their bodies. The moment when she'd whispered "I love you," and he'd never answered…because he wanted it too much.

But how could he drag her any deeper into the tangle that was his life?

Please…let me fix this.

There was no certainty that she would want a life with him, that there was any future they could ever share. He didn't understand her world, and he worried about the cost to her of getting involved with his.

But, whispered that tiny seed, *there is no chance if you don't try.*

He lifted his head and focused on the card in his mother's hand.

He looked at Albert Manning. "Are you sure my mother can come out clean?"

"It's not my field, son, but Callie swears it's true. She plans to do everything in her power to make it happen, including devoting every cent of Miss Margaret's inheritance if that's necessary."

Oh, God. Not only her career but her financial future on the line. How could he possibly—

Lean on me, she'd asked on that magical night. Depending on anyone else went against every instinct in him.

But he knew what lay down that road of isolation, so he extended his hand for the phone, and began to dial.

WHEN HER CELL PHONE RANG, Callie was closing an old suitcase of Miss Margaret's. She'd intended to leave two hours ago, but instead she kept wandering the house, picking up this knickknack or that, gazing out over the garden, wondering how all this would fare when it was vacant.

She thought over her late-night conversation with Albert Manning and the steps she'd outlined for him to follow once he'd spoken to David, while trying not to imagine how angry David would be.

"Hello?"

A long pause. "Callie?"

Her eyes went wide. "David?" She gripped the wing chair beside the front window.

Another silence ensued, one she was afraid to puncture. She had no idea what to say to him after the way they'd parted.

"How sure are you that you can get my mother off without any jail time?"

Her heart took a little skip. "Very. And I'm waiting for a friend to call with a recommendation for a good defense attorney."

"Where are you now?"

"Now?" she echoed. "Um…I was just loading the car."

"You're still in Oak Hollow?"

She waited for the explosion.

None came. "Would you…could you drive over here instead?"

Callie closed her eyes. Covered her mouth. After a minute she managed to speak. "Yes."

"Just like that, yes? No questions?"

She shook her head, then realized he couldn't see her. "No—yes. Are you going to let me help you, too?"

"That doesn't matter so much. It's my mother I'm worried about."

"It does matter, David. *You* matter," she insisted. "You're important to me."

"Did you mean it?" His voice lowered as if he might have an audience. "When you said that you loved me?"

"Yes." She was afraid to hope he felt the same. Maybe she just had to be content with this beginning.

"It's crazy. I can't see how we can fit. I mean, you have your life there and your career while I—"

The climb from the depths where he was mired must seem insurmountable, she realized. "My life in Philly isn't much, David." Saying it out loud, she realized it was really true. From the moment her boss had exiled her, a process had begun to crack her blindness about the barren life she'd been living. Coming to Oak Hollow, getting involved with its people, finding David again—all had contributed to widening the crack and making her see how one-dimensional her life had been.

"I shouldn't like hearing that, but I do." There was a small smile in his tone.

Her heart which had been leaden and gray, suddenly soared.

"Callie, I'm sorry I hurt you." He paused. "I did it because I was trying not to drag you down with me, but—"

She sagged onto the chair arm as relief swept over her. "I have much more to apologize for. If you'd never met me, none of this would have happened. Everything you've suffered began with me."

"No. Don't say that. You were just a mixed-up kid. Ned Compton is the villain of this piece." His voice lowered to an intimate murmur. "Look, I—we need to talk, but not like this."

The forgiveness she heard had her eyes burning. "Let Albert do his magic with the judge, okay?" She cleared her throat. "And tell him I'm on my way."

She raced from the house and jumped into her car,

holding on to the phone as if it would keep her connected to David and to the future she wanted so badly to share.

SHE MADE THE HOUR TRIP in considerably less.

She'd left her suitcase at home...or what felt more like home than any place she'd ever lived. *We need to talk.* She imagined they would have a great deal to discuss before all this was over.

But that was the question, wasn't it? Would whatever this was between them be over once he was free? Was she crazy for thinking past the tangle David and his mother were in?

Her phone rang just then. She glanced at the display, expecting it to be David or Albert or even Delia.

When her office number appeared on the display, she nearly didn't answer. *Not now, not when my mind is so full of him...when there's so much on the line.* But she answered. "Hello?"

"Where the hell are you?" asked Joe Santiago, her friend and advocate.

"Hello to you, too, Joe." The tension in his tone wasn't encouraging. "I'm in Georgia."

"Still? Never mind. You need to get back here, Callie. Things are heating up."

Dread filled her. "By things, you mean me. My witness."

"That reporter, Tim Caraway, he's not letting go, Cal. The D.A.'s getting cold feet. If you want your job, you'd better remind him about why he hired you in the first place."

"Gerald ordered me to make myself scarce."

"I know, but you can't afford to listen. Not now."

"He was pretty clear, Joe. Out of sight, out of mind."

"You never backed down from a fight before. What's up?"

She wasn't backing down now. But it occurred to her she might be choosing a different battle. "I can't really leave yet."

"What? Funeral's over, right?"

"Yes, but there are…complications."

"No, not now—" he interrupted, obviously talking to someone else. "I'll be there in a sec." His voice came back. "Sorry, Cal. What did you say?" He sounded harried. Running ninety miles an hour, as usual, and loving every second.

She used to get a rush from it, too. Her eyes widened. *Used to*—had she really thought that?

"Callie?"

She shook her head to clear it. "Joe, I'm losing the signal," she dodged. "I'd better go." *Don't do anything hasty. Don't.*

"Cal, are you coming or not?"

"I'll call you back, Joe, when I can." Before she could change her mind, she disconnected.

The last few blocks before the jail, she tried to picture herself back in the middle of that adrenaline-fueled existence where the dregs of humanity rubbed grime on her soul daily, only she hadn't realized how dingy her world had become until she'd been faced with green mountains and crystal blue skies. There were problems here, yes—

she only had to bring Mickey Patton or Ned Compton to mind—but there were also folks like Granny Chambers and Albert Manning and Luella Sims…

And David Langley. A hero once again.

She parked her car and rubbed sweaty palms on her thighs before getting out. Part of her was jubilant that he seemed to be giving her a chance.

Part of her was terrified of letting him down.

You can do this, you know you can.

But then what? What happened if she did get him cleared? What did she do about Philly? When he was free, what would he choose?

As she made her way down the hall to the interview room, she was more nervous than she could recall being in years.

And then she saw him, standing there with his hands bound. She was relieved to note that the two of them were alone at least. In some ways it felt as if they were meeting for the first time, only so many shadows hovered in the background.

She ventured one glance at his eyes.

Mossy-green. Soft. Looking as uncertain as she felt.

For once in her life, Callie had no words.

Still, there was touch. She crossed to him, took his shackled hands in hers, and realized that the simplest words were the most right. "Thank you."

His eyebrows rose. "Thank you?"

"For giving me a chance. For letting me help you. I know it's not easy." She halted when he squeezed her hands and lowered his head to hers.

"What's not easy," he said in a low, intimate tone that gave her the shivers, "is standing here like this, when I want so badly to hold you."

All the air escaped from her lungs. "Really?" She blinked hard. "I won't let you down, David, I promise. I'm good at what I do."

His expression turned carefully blank. "What about your job? Don't you need to get back there?"

He was looking out for her again. She sighed. "You're not the only one who hasn't been forthcoming. I'm not really sure I have a job to go back to."

"But you might? If you didn't hang around?"

"I honestly don't know, and I'm not sure I care." She stilled with the shock of saying the words out loud.

"Callie, you don't have to do this."

"Hush." She really didn't know if she cared about saving the life she'd left. "Right now the important question is, do you trust me, David? Will you place your future in my hands?" She braced for his response, clear just how huge such a request was for him.

He took his time answering, searching her face thoroughly. But he never let go of her. "I trust you as much as I've ever trusted anyone," he said. "I'm realizing that some of what happened to me was because I thought I had to be some kind of hero."

"You are a hero, David. And not just to me."

He looked away for a minute, then caught her eyes with his tender expression. "It's hard, Callie, I won't lie to you about that. I don't trust much anymore, but I do believe in you, and—" He cleared his throat. "I don't want to say I love you for the first time while standing in a jail."

A smile rose like morning inside her. She gripped his hands more tightly and didn't even try for composure. "You don't have to." She waggled her eyebrows playfully. "But I'd sure like to hear it as soon as I get you out."

"Then hurry up, lawyer lady." He smiled back, slow and sweet and tempting. "'Cause that's not all I plan to do once I'm out."

Callie didn't want to go, but she wanted much more to have him all to herself, to begin the process of setting David Langley free to choose whatever future he wanted.

"I can't tell you exactly how long it will take," she said, "but I won't rest one second until then, I swear."

His big hands surrounded hers, and she clung just as hard.

At last he let go. Stepped back, eyes locked on hers with both hope and promise in them. "I'll be waiting, sweetheart. You be careful."

"You, too." She devoured him with her gaze.

Walking out of there without him was the hardest thing she'd ever done.

She stopped in the doorway and blew him a kiss. Watched those serious eyes hold her like a caress.

Then Lady Justice rolled up her sleeves, donned her most lethal stilettos and went to work.

CHAPTER NINETEEN

MICKEY PATTON DIDN'T BUDGE on his version of events.

Not that David was surprised.

Others at the bar that night did, though, as did Patton's flunky Stanley about the second assault accusation, after Callie made it her business to be sure everyone in Oak Hollow knew that David had never killed anyone, that who they'd believed he was as a boy had been the truth.

Now, however, he knew himself to be a different person, one who couldn't quite catch up to the notion that he was free. Callie had organized the dizzying parade of legal procedures, Albert Manning had pitched in and Randy Capwell had returned to town in time to help get all the charges against him dropped.

He still had a criminal record, but the process of obtaining a pardon from the governor was under way. More importantly, Callie had spoken, prosecutor to prosecutor, to the D.A. with a convincing argument that his mother's case was not worth pursuing.

Suddenly the citizens of Oak Hollow could not do enough for him. Had he wanted to, he could become mayor, could have a job anywhere he wished, could ask for practically anything he wanted.

But all he wanted was Callie.

"You were supposed to sleep late," she accused in a sleepy voice. "We celebrated half the night."

He rolled onto his side and studied her. "It's my first day as a free man. I don't want to waste it." He reached out, brushed a tousled curl from her eyes. "How do I begin to thank you, Callie? I..." He shrugged one shoulder, completely at a loss.

She placed one slender finger against his mouth. "You don't have to. It was my very great pleasure." Then her solemn tone turned to teasing. "Although I could think of a thing or two we haven't tried yet..."

He shouldn't let her make light of it. If it took the rest of his life, he would keep trying to tell her what it meant that she hadn't given up on him when he'd thought his life was over.

"You've got that serious look again," she said. "What am I going to do with—"

"I love you so much," he interrupted. "Callie, I want to spend my life with you. I don't know how, I don't know where...I have no education to fall back on, no idea what kind of job I could get." He gathered her to him. "But I'll love you with everything in me. I'll work hard, and I'm smart. I'll make up lost ground if it's the last thing I do." She snuggled into him, and he said a silent prayer that he be allowed to make her life all that even a windmill-tilting boy had never dared to dream.

"I think you should go to college. Or focus on your woodcarving," she murmured, right before she swirled her tongue over his ear.

"What?" He lost her words in the surge of physical response to what was still so new, so overwhelming.

She rose and straddled him, let the quilt they'd bundled into last night fall from her shoulders. As she swiveled her hips and sent his mind reeling, she gave him a huge smile, punctuating each word with a gentle poke of her fingernail against his chest. "College. Beautiful carvings of wood."

"You're kidding." His head spun. He couldn't possibly.

"Do you not know how talented you are?"

He hadn't dared to imagine so much for a very long time. "Where would I do it, Philadelphia?"

A shake of her head. "I don't live in Philadelphia anymore."

His eyes narrowed. He captured the hands that were stroking. Tormenting. "Stop that. What do you mean you don't live there?"

"I'm a woman of property, you see." She smiled. "I don't need that job."

He thought he saw shadows. "But you loved it."

The eyes grew fierce. "I lived for it. It was all I had. That's not healthy." She bent to him. "I love *you,* not my career."

"But you're good at the law, Callie. You can't just— you don't want to live in Oak Hollow, surely."

"Why not? At least I do if you're here." Uncertainty burgeoned. "That is, I thought we…"

"You thought right." He pulled her down, cuddled her. "If you mean that, I'm not letting you out of my sight."

She nestled in. "That's good."

"But you won't be happy simply being a landlord, don't give me that. If you leave your job, what will that do to your career prospects?"

"It doesn't matter," she said in small voice.

He knew it did. "Albert Manning wants to retire, and folks around here will need a good lawyer. Or I heard Randy Capwell ask if you'd like to set up a practice with him. Would those be too big a comedown from being Lady Justice?"

Her smile was wry. "I like *lawyer lady* better. You get me hot when you say that."

"Be serious, Callie. Oak Hollow's not important to me." He stared off into the distance, wondered how the beauty of the place compared with the taint of recent history.

"I think it is," she said, tilting her head back to look at him. "And I've found that I have a taste for the other side of the table. I liked defending you and your mom. But that's not the issue. What do you want to do?"

He pondered the wealth of options he might have, the dizzying freedom of choices. "I have to earn my own way. I'm not living off you."

She smiled. "You won't. We'll both live off Miss Margaret's bounty. If we stayed here, we'd have a house free and clear plus some income every month. If we don't, there's still the money coming in."

"That's yours, not mine."

She sat up. Poked him again. "Don't give me that. Miss Margaret adored you. You never gave her a bit of trouble, which is more than you can say about me."

"She didn't leave all this to me, Callie."

Her look was sly. "Well, then, I guess you'll just have to make an honest woman of me so I'll share."

She drove him crazy, that wily brain of hers. "I intend to."

Callie grew serious. "You really mean it, don't you?"

"Dead serious." He sat up, too. "Callie, I want to make a family with you."

"But what about college? Or your art? Or both? You could even travel, and—"

He hushed her with a kiss that turned quickly carnal. When she was writhing against him, he dredged up the last bits of control. "I swear I never met anyone who loved to argue any more than you." When she narrowed her eyes at him, he stroked down her body, rewarded by her gasp.

"There's no reason we can't manage all of it, lawyer lady." He gazed at this woman who was his miracle. "You're smart, I'm smart. We both work hard. And we'll make incredible babies…." He fell silent as their gazes met and the tragedy of those long-ago years shimmered between them.

"Maybe we shouldn't—" she began, shadows stealing over them again.

"You were too young, honey. Your body wasn't ready. We'll be fine, I really believe that. If you're willing, that is. If you're not, that's okay. You're what matters." He touched his forehead to hers. "I'm ready to take chances, my love. How about you? Gamble on a beat-up old ex-con?"

Her smile was tremulous, but her eyes warmed with hope. "The only crime you're guilty of," she said, stroking his jaw, "is stealing my heart."

"Do the crime, do the time." He held out his wrists. "Lock me up, lawyer lady, and throw away the key." He bent to kiss her. To love her, to hold her for the rest of their lives.

Thankful to his marrow for every day of pain, every heartache, every bump in the rough road that had brought her back to him.

* * * * *

*Celebrate 60 years of pure reading pleasure
with Harlequin®!*

To commemorate the event, Silhouette Special
Edition invites you to Ashley O'Ballivan's bed-
and-breakfast in the small town of Stone Creek.
The beautiful innkeeper will have her hands full
caring for her old flame Jack McCall. He's on the
run and recovering from a mysterious illness, but
that won't stop him from trying to win Ashley back.

*Enjoy an exclusive glimpse of Linda Lael Miller's
AT HOME IN STONE CREEK
Available in November 2009 from
Silhouette Special Edition®*

The helicopter swung abruptly sideways in a dizzying arch, setting Jack McCall's fever-ravaged brain spinning.

His friend's voice sounded tinny, coming through the earphones. "You belong in a hospital," he said. "Not some backwater bed-and-breakfast."

All Jack really knew about the virus raging through his system was that it wasn't contagious, and there was no known treatment for it besides a lot of rest and quiet. "I don't like hospitals," he responded, hoping he sounded like his normal self. "They're full of sick people."

Vince Griffin chuckled but it was a dry sound, rough at the edges. "What's in Stone Creek, Arizona?" he asked. "Besides a whole lot of nothin'?"

Ashley O'Ballivan was in Stone Creek, and she was a whole lot of somethin', but Jack had neither the strength nor the inclination to explain. After the way he'd ducked out six months before, he didn't expect a welcome, knew he didn't deserve one. But Ashley, being Ashley, would take him in whatever her misgivings.

He had to get to Ashley; he'd be all right.

He closed his eyes, letting the fever swallow him.

There was no telling how much time had passed when he became aware of the chopper blades slowing overhead. Dimly, he saw the private ambulance waiting on the airfield outside of Stone Creek; it seemed that twilight had descended.

Jack sighed with relief. His clothes felt clammy against his flesh. His teeth began to chatter as two figures unloaded a gurney from the back of the ambulance and waited for the blades to stop.

"Great," Vince remarked, unsnapping his seat belt. "Those two look like volunteers, not real EMTs."

The chopper bounced sickeningly on its runners, and Vince, with a shake of his head, pushed open his door and jumped to the ground, head down.

Jack waited, wondering if he'd be able to stand on his own. After fumbling unsuccessfully with the buckle on his seat belt, he decided not.

When it was safe the EMTs approached, following Vince, who opened Jack's door.

His old friend Tanner Quinn stepped around Vince, his grin not quite reaching his eyes.

"You look like hell warmed over," he told Jack cheerfully.

"Since when are you an EMT?" Jack retorted.

Tanner reached in, wedged a shoulder under Jack's right arm and hauled him out of the chopper. His knees immediately buckled, and Vince stepped up, supporting him on the other side.

"In a place like Stone Creek," Tanner replied, "everybody helps out."

They reached the wheeled gurney, and Jack found himself on his back.

Tanner and the second man strapped him down, a process that brought back a few bad memories.

"Is there even a hospital in this place?" Vince asked irritably from somewhere in the night.

"There's a pretty good clinic over in Indian Rock," Tanner answered easily, "and it isn't far to Flagstaff." He paused to help his buddy hoist Jack and the gurney into the back of the ambulance. "You're in good hands, Jack. My wife is the best veterinarian in the state."

Jack laughed raggedly at that.

Vince muttered a curse.

Tanner climbed into the back beside him, perched on some kind of fold-down seat. The other man shut the doors.

"You in any pain?" Tanner said as his partner climbed into the driver's seat and started the engine.

"No." Jack looked up at his oldest and closest friend and wished he'd listened to Vince. Ever since he'd come down with the virus—a week after snatching a five-year-old girl back from her non-custodial parent, a small-time Colombian drug dealer—he hadn't been able to think about anyone or anything but Ashley. When he *could* think, anyway.

Now, in one of the first clearheaded moments he'd experienced since checking himself out of Bethesda the day before, he realized he might be making a major mistake. Not by facing Ashley—he owed her that much and a lot more. No, he could be putting her in danger, putting Tanner and his daughter and his pregnant wife in danger, too.

"I shouldn't have come here," he said, keeping his voice low.

Tanner shook his head, his jaw clamped down hard as though he was irritated by Jack's statement.

"This is where you belong," Tanner insisted. "If you'd had sense enough to know that six months ago, old buddy, when you bailed on Ashley without so much as a fare-thee-well, you wouldn't be in this mess."

Ashley. The name had run through his mind a million times in those six months, but hearing somebody say it out loud was like having a fist close around his insides and squeeze hard.

Jack couldn't speak.

Tanner didn't press for further conversation.

The ambulance bumped over country roads, finally hitting smooth blacktop.

"Here we are," Tanner said. "Ashley's place."

* * * * *

Will Jack be able to patch things up with Ashley,
or will his past put the woman he loves
in harm's way?
Find out in
AT HOME IN STONE CREEK
by Linda Lael Miller
Available November 2009 from
Silhouette Special Edition®

This November,
Silhouette Special Edition®
brings you

NEW YORK TIMES
BESTSELLING AUTHOR

LINDA LAEL
MILLER

At Home in
Stone Creek

Available in November
wherever books are sold.

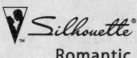

Romantic
SUSPENSE

**Sparked by Danger,
Fueled by Passion.**

Blackout At Christmas

Beth Cornelison,
Sharron McClellan,
Jennifer Morey

What happens when a major blackout shuts
down the entire Western seaboard on Christmas
Eve? Follow stories of danger, intrigue and
romance as three women learn to trust their
instincts to survive and open their hearts to the
love that unexpectedly comes their way.

**Available November
wherever books are sold.**

Visit Silhouette Books at www.eHarlequin.com

SRS27653

HARLEQUIN *Romance*

This November,
queen of the rugged rancher

PATRICIA
THAYER

teams up with

DONNA ALWARD

to bring you an extra-special treat
this holiday season—

two romantic stories
in one book!

Join sisters Amelia and Kelley for Christmas at
Rocking H Ranch where these feisty cowgirls swap
presents for proposals, mistletoe for marriage and
experience the unbeatable rush of falling in love!

Available in November wherever books are sold.

REQUEST YOUR FREE BOOKS!

2 FREE NOVELS PLUS 2 FREE GIFTS!

HARLEQUIN®

Super Romance®

Exciting, emotional, unexpected!

YES! Please send me 2 FREE Harlequin® Superromance® novels and my 2 FREE gifts (gifts are worth about $10). After receiving them, if I don't wish to receive any more books, I can return the shipping statement marked "cancel." If I don't cancel, I will receive 6 brand-new novels every month and be billed just $4.69 per book in the U.S. or $5.24 per book in Canada. That's a savings of close to 15% off the cover price! It's quite a bargain! Shipping and handling is just 50¢ per book*. I understand that accepting the 2 free books and gifts places me under no obligation to buy anything. I can always return a shipment and cancel at any time. Even if I never buy another book from Harlequin, the two free books and gifts are mine to keep forever.

135 HDN EYLG   336 HDN EYLS

Name _____ (PLEASE PRINT) _____

Address _____ Apt. # _____

City _____ State/Prov. _____ Zip/Postal Code _____

Signature (if under 18, a parent or guardian must sign)

Mail to the **Harlequin Reader Service:**
IN U.S.A.: P.O. Box 1867, Buffalo, NY 14240-1867
IN CANADA: P.O. Box 609, Fort Erie, Ontario L2A 5X3

Not valid to current subscribers of Harlequin Superromance books.

**Are you a current subscriber of Harlequin Superromance books
and want to receive the larger-print edition?
Call 1-800-873-8635 today!**

* Terms and prices subject to change without notice. Prices do not include applicable taxes. Sales tax applicable in N.Y. Canadian residents will be charged applicable provincial taxes and GST. Offer not valid in Quebec. This offer is limited to one order per household. All orders subject to approval. Credit or debit balances in a customer's account(s) may be offset by any other outstanding balance owed by or to the customer. Please allow 4 to 6 weeks for delivery. Offer available while quantities last.

Your Privacy: Harlequin is committed to protecting your privacy. Our Privacy Policy is available online at www.eHarlequin.com or upon request from the Reader Service. From time to time we make our lists of customers available to reputable third parties who may have a product or service of interest to you. If you would prefer we not share your name and address, please check here. ☐

HSR09R

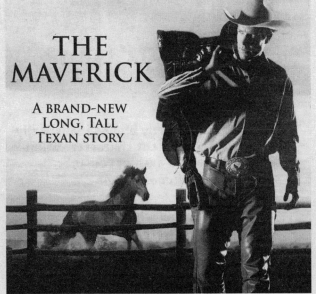

Silhouette Desire

**FROM *NEW YORK TIMES*
BESTSELLING AUTHOR**

DIANA
PALMER

THE
MAVERICK

**A BRAND-NEW
LONG, TALL
TEXAN STORY**

HARLEQUIN
Ambassadors

*Want to share your passion
for reading Harlequin® Books?*

Become a Harlequin Ambassador!

Harlequin Ambassadors are a group
of passionate and well-connected readers
who are willing to share their joy of reading
Harlequin® books with family and friends.

You'll be sent all the tools you need to spark
great conversation, including free books!

All we ask is that you share the romance
with your friends and family!

You'll also be invited to have a say in
new book ideas and exchange opinions
with women just like you!

**To see if you qualify* to be
a Harlequin Ambassador, please visit
www.HarlequinAmbassadors.com.**

*Please note that not everyone who applies to be a Harlequin Ambassador will
qualify. For more information please visit www.HarlequinAmbassadors.com.

Thank you for your participation.

BAP09BPA

COMING NEXT MONTH

Available November 10, 2009

#1596 LIKE FATHER, LIKE SON • Karina Bliss
The Diamond Legacy
What's worse? Discovering his heritage is a lie or following in his grandfather's
footsteps? All Joe Fraser *does* know is that Philippa Browne is pregnant and he's
got to do right by her. Too bad she has her own ideas about motherhood…and marriage.

#1597 HER SECRET RIVAL • Abby Gaines
Those Merritt Girls
Taking over her father's law firm isn't just the professional opportunity of a lifetime—
it's a chance for Megan Merritt to finally get close to him. Winning a lucrative divorce
case is her way to prove she's the one for the job. Except the opposing lawyer in the
divorce is Travis Jamieson, who is also after her dad's job!

#1598 A CONFLICT OF INTEREST • Anna Adams
Welcome to Honesty
Jake Sloane knows right from wrong—as a judge, it's his responsibility. Until he meets
Maria Keaton, he's never blurred that line. Now his attraction to her is tearing him
between what his head knows he should do and what his heart wants.

#1599 HOME FOR THE HOLIDAYS • Sarah Mayberry
Single Father
Raising his kids on his own is a huge learning curve for Joe Lawson. So does he really
have time to fall for the unconventional woman next door, Hannah Napier? Time or no,
that's what's happening.…

#1600 A MAN WORTH LOVING • Kimberly Van Meter
Home in Emmett's Mill
Aubrey Rose can't stand Sammy Halvorsen when they first meet. She agrees to be a
nanny to his infant son only because she's a sucker for babies. As she gets to know
Sammy, however, she starts to fall for him. But how to make him realize he's a man
worth loving?

#1601 UNEXPECTED GIFTS • Holly Jacobs
9 Months Later
Elinore Cartright has her hands full overseeing the teen parenting program, especially
when she discovers *she's* unexpectedly expecting. Not how she envisioned her
forties, but life's unpredictable. So is her friend Zac Keller, who suddenly wants to date
her *and* be a daddy, too!